Phoenix Young Readers Library

Anna the Air Hostess

Phoenix Young Readers Library

1.	Lots of Wonders	Sam Mbure
2.	The Sun and the Wind	Anne Matindi
3.	The Pet Snake	Dickson Mukunyi
4.	The Greedy Host	J.K. Njoroge
5.	The Speck of Gold	Cynthia Hunter
6.	The Peacock and the Snake	Elijah K. Soi
7.	The Return of Njaga	Joel Makumi
8.	Beautiful Nyakio	Frederick Ndungu
9.	Teddy Mapesa and the Missing Cash	Hillary Namunyu
10.	Mzee Nyachote	Roeland Japuojo
11.	The Fly Whisk	Stephen Gichuru
12.	The Talking Devil	Leo Odera Omolo
13.	The Feather in the Lake	Joel Makumi
14.	Give the Devil his Due	W.K. Boruett
15.	Inspector Rajabu Investigates	F. Kawegere
16.	The Powerful Magician	Daniel Irungu
17	End of the Beginning	Joel Makumi
18	Onyango's Triumph	Leo Odera Omolo
19	Tales of Wamugumo	Peter N. Kuguru
20.	The Girl Who Couldn't Keep a Secret	Clare Omanga
21.	Wake Up and Open Your Eyes	Edward Muhire
22.	Njaga and the Safari Rally	Joel Makumi
23.	Njogu the Prophet	Jamlick Mutua
24.	Travels of a Raindrop	David Ng'osos
25.	The Adventurers of Thiga	C M. Mureithi
26.	Pamela the Probation Officer	Cynthia Hunter
27.	Anna the Air Hostess	Cynthia Hunter
28.	The Circle of Revenge	David Mwaurah
29.	Town Tricksters	David Mwaurah
30.	Truphena Student Nurse	Cynthia Hunter
31.	Truphena City Nurse	Cynthia Hunter
32.	The River Without Frogs	Writers' Committee
33.	The Great Siege of Fort Jesus	Valerie Cuthbert
34.	Captured by Raiders	Banjamin S. Wegesa
35.	Njaga the Town Monkey	Joel Makumi
36.	Njaga Returns to the village	Joel Makumi

and more .... many more

Anna the Air Hostess

Cynthia E. Hunter

PHŒNIX PUBLISHERS, NAIROBI

First published in 1967
First Phoenix edition published in 1989 by
Phoenix Publishers Ltd.
Grain Belt Industrial Park,
Sukari Industrial Estate,
Off Thika Road, Behind Clay Works,
P.O. Box 30474-00100,
Nairobi.

ISBN 9966 47 098 0

Reprinted in 1989, 1990, 1992, 1996, 1998, 2001, 2003, 2006,
2008, 2010, 2011, 2013, 2017, 2021

To those who fly

Contents

Chapter 1

THE CHOSEN FEW

Anna had always lived in a far-off world of her own. Her parents often wondered what went on in her mind. At times they fussed over her; at times they worried. How could two ordinary people have such a strange daughter?

"She'll come to no good, that one," the women often said to Anna's mother, as they walked slowly home from the fields, bent under the weight of enormous loads of firewood. "You marry her off quickly or you'll have trouble with her. Marriage will bring her down to earth."

Jonathan had been, the same, but then he was their eldest, and a boy — boys were different! His early promise was reaching fulfilment; he had passed all his exams with exceptional brilliance and now, at the age of twenty-three, was representing his country overseas as a junior member of the Diplomatic Service.

At the end of Standard Seven, Anna had passed her primary school leaving exam, and, although she had not known her exact marks, the teachers had hinted that she had set a record in the high standard she had attained. Her father thought she was really too clever for a girl, and decided she had better leave school and help her mother with the domestic chores which would fit her for home life and marriage.

He had not reckoned with the horrified expression on the Headmaster's face when he suggested this in answer to a question about Anna's future.

"But, but..." The headmaster nearly exploded. Then he gained control of himself. "You must understand, Mr. Lumwaji," he said quietly. "Your daughter is no ordinary girl. She's by far the most outstanding pupil we've had in this school for many years. I'd like to recommend her for St. Mary's High School. She can be a boarder there."

It was Anna's father's turn to show his feelings!

"But I can't possibly pay boarding fees for Anna," he almost shouted at the Headmaster. "I've four other children to feed and clothe and educate."

"Think it over," said the headmaster, calmly. "Let me put her name forward. She's a good chance of obtaining a scholarship and then you won't have to pay very much."

Anna's father went home after the interview, marvelling how he had been blessed with such a clever son and daughter. When he reached the house, he was greeted by a messenger from the Post Office bringing a letter from Jonathan. He handed the letter to his second son, Elijah, and asked him to read it aloud.

"Dear Father," wrote Jonathan. "I hope you and all the family are well. It is very cold here and this time of the year it gets dark at about three o'clock in the afternoon.

My work keeps me busy but I've made lots of friends and we've formed a group which we call the 'Africa Club'. People from all parts of Africa meet once a week and talk about our homes and discuss all sorts of things which affect our countries.

2

Anna has written to tell me that she stands a good chance of going on to a Secondary Boarding School, so I'm sending a money order for a thousand shillings to help pay her fees. You must let her go; she's such a clever girl and she should get a well-paid and interesting job if she has a good education – and marry someone in a good position!

Please send my greetings to mother and all the family.

Your son,

Jonathan."

"Well!" exclaimed Anna's father, holding the paper, which, to him, represented the savings of a life-time, tightly in his hand. "That settles the matter!"

Anna came home for the holidays and helped her mother in the house, but she often escaped with some books she had borrowed from school and found a shady grove near the edge of the forest. There she lay and read about foreign countries and dreamt of the time when she would be able to visit them.

One afternoon, five weeks after the end of term, the Post Office messenger again called at their house. This time he held up a pink envelope.

"Postmaster says you've been accepted at St Mary's High School," he said to Anna, who greeted him by the door of her hut.

Anna, momentarily forgetting her manners, almost snatched the telegram from the messenger's hands. She remembered, just in time, to thank him for bringing it, before she rushed round to her father who was smoking his pipe in the back yard.

"Open it, Father, open it," she cried excitedly.

Her father took the envelope and pulled out the paper with the white ribbon of print pasted across it.

"You read it," he said, handing it to Anna.

"ANNA OFFERED PLACE AT HIGH SCHOOL. BRING SOON AS POSSIBLE," she read.

She rushed off to tell her mother and then started to pack her few possessions into her little case, wondering how she was going to get to Nairobi. When she had finished, she went outside and found her mother and father talking to one of their neighbours.

"Timona says that the bus from the village will take you to Masingu and from there you can get a seat in a taxi going to town. For an extra shilling, the driver will take you right up to the school."

The next day Anna travelled the long road to the city. Near the end of the journey, she heard the roar of a plane above the purr of the taxi's engine. She looked out of the window and saw a huge aircraft flying over the edge of the city towards the airport. Intense excitement welled up inside her as she realized that her acceptance at the High School was a step towards achieving her secret ambition to become an air hostess. She had made up her mind that this was to be her future career, ever since that day, a year ago, she had stood at the 'waving-base' at the airport and had watched her brother Jonathan fly off to England.

Although boarding school was a completely new experience for Anna, she accepted the routine and joined in with the life of the school as if she had been brought up knowing what it was like. As one term followed another, she was always top or near the top of the class, and like her brother she passed exams, easily. She read the newspapers and journals provided by the school and gained a sound knowledge of current affairs by listening regularly to the news on the wireless. She took a great interest in events occurring in all parts of the world.

In the second form, she was elected a prefect. She also joined the committee of the Musical Society and was elected President of the Debating Society; she was a member of both the Netball and Hockey teams and was one of the most popular girls in the school.

At the end of her last term in Form Four, Anna sat for her School Certificate. Before the exams, people from many different professions came to talk to the girls in order to help them decide on their future careers. Anna sat patiently through talks on Teaching, Nursing and Secretarial work but she found nothing to interest her. At last she was rewarded when one morning a good-looking, middle-aged man walked into the hall and was introduced as the Chief Training Officer from the Airport!

Tom Clinton was wearing a well-cut, dark blue suit, a white shirt and a dark blue tie. Under his arm he carried a blue peaked cap with a gold badge on the front. On the shoulders of his jacket, there were two narrow gold stripes. He walked confidently across the platform and stood for a moment looking at the sea of eager faces turned towards him.

"It's hot in here," he began. "You girls won't mind if I take off my jacket, will you?"

He did so, and Anna noticed the two narrow gold stripes were repeated on the shoulders of his shirt.

As Tom Clinton smiled down at the girls, his expression was kind and understanding.

"Now, I expect when you see me, you think I'm only here to talk about the work of an Air Hostess, but first I'm going to tell you about all the other jobs connected with the Airlines. Remember, many more ground staff than crew are needed to keep a plane in the air. Those who actually fly form only a small proportion of all the personnel at the Airport. Think of the engineers, mechanics, painters, traffic controllers and radio officers, ground stewards and stewardesses, clerks and caterers, to mention only a few."

He went on to give an outline of the work that girls could do on the ground'.

Anna, who had at first sat back, hoping the time would go quickly until the speaker started telling them about the work of an Air Hostess, found she was leaning forward, fascinated, as Tom Clinton described the many kinds of work that needed to be done at the Airport, apart from flying duties.

"Oh well," she thought. "If I don't become an Air Hostess, there's still a lot of other things I can do. 'Ground Hostess', for instance; I'd meet all the passengers in that job."

She was trying to persuade herself that she would not be too disappointed if she did not pass the tests and interviews, but she knew in her heart that to be an Air Hostess was the job of her dreams and she would be satisfied with nothing less.

"Now for the work you are all waiting to hear about," said Tom Clinton. Although he already had their interest, there was a slight murmur of expectation as the girls leant forward to hear about one of the most glamorous jobs in the world.

"The first thing you should know is that there are thousands and thousands of applications from girls who want to be Air Hostesses, but only about two or three out of five hundred are taken on; sometimes even one of these fails to complete the course. The work is glamorous and exciting but it can also be tedious and tiring. Over half your time is spent serving food and drinks. Your first duty is to children, babies and old people — not to the good-looking, wealthy business-men," he added with a smile.

A few giggles were heard in the audience.

"He's trying to put us off," whispered Anna to her next-door neighbour.

"Another disadvantage is that your social life is never your own," continued Tom Clinton. "You might be getting ready to go to your best friend's party when you are told to fly to the other end of the earth! On the other hand, there's also the chance that you might suddenly be called on to fly to London and will be there to attend your brother's wedding. That actually happened to a girl last week!"

The girls gasped — the very thought of suddenly being whisked off half-way round the world at a moment's notice was thrilling.

"I can tell that you still think it's a wonderful job," continued the Chief Training Officer. "But believe me, there are snags! You can be held up for hours at airports because of bad weather or engine trouble; then you have to pacify angry passengers who see their night's sleep or, worse still, their business opportunities, slipping away. You fly from a hot climate to a cold one; you often lose hours of sleep and have to be on duty at any time of the day or night. And you have to remain good-tempered and helpful no matter how tired you feel. The passenger, like the customer, is always right!"

"So now you realize why no one is considered unless they are a hundred per cent physically fit, besides being friendly, intelligent, charming and tactful. If you think you have all those qualities, then you are the right person to apply for the position of Air Hostess with our Airline."

Tom Clinton stopped talking and there was a moment's silence before the long burst of applause. Anna looked up and, for a brief moment, found herself staring straight into a pair of deep-set, blue eyes. Tom's face crinkled in a kindly smile.

"I'll leave application forms for all the jobs I have mentioned with your Headmistress," he said. "Good luck to you," he added as he finally turned away.

The girls sat in silence, thinking about all the exciting jobs that had been described. Then a loud chattering broke out as they made their way back to their classroom.

The next day, Anna went to the Headmistress's office and asked to fill in an application form for an Air Hostess.

"Why do you think you are suited to this particular job?" asked the Head. "We were all hoping you would stay on for sixth form work and take your H.S.C."

"I've always wanted to fly," said Anna. "Ever since I saw my brother off to England and he wrote and told me about his flight. He went while I was still at Primary School!"

"Well, here's the form," said the Headmistress. "Fill it in and I'll forward it for you with a recommendation. You won't be finally accepted until your School Certificate results are out. If you like, you can come back next term and study a language and do Domestic Science and First Aid — those subjects will be very useful to you if your mind is set on being an Air Hostess."

Anna thanked her and took the form away and filled it in very carefully.

School Certificate exams, came and went. About two days before the end of term, the Headmistress called Anna and nine other girls and told them they were to go to the Town Hall the following day for an exam, and an interview by a 'panel' from the Airline.

The exam, turned out to be a 'General Knowledge' test, and to any one with a lively, intelligent mind like Anna, it presented no problems. The interview, by three officials from the Airport, was in much the same vein.

It was early in the next term that the Headmistress again called Anna to her study. "Many apply but few are chosen," she said with a smile. "You've been called for an interview at the Airport. You're the only one who has been picked for an Air Hostess, although some others have been offered Ground Staff duties."

It was not far to the Airport and on the appointed day, the Headmistress herself saw Anna on to the bus and instructed her exactly where to go.

Anna found her way through a maze of buildings to a small office marked 'Chief Steward'. She knocked timidly.

"Come in," said a pleasant voice.

She opened the door and there was the Chief Training Officer, Tom Clinton, smiling up at her from his desk. For the second time, his deep blue eyes held her own clear brown ones as if he could read her innermost thoughts.

An aircraft flew low over the building as a knock on the door heralded the entrance of Miss Symonds, the Chief Stewardess, and Mr. Ngugi, one of the airline officials who had been at Anna's previous interview. After the first few questions, Anna found she was actually enjoying herself and talking quite naturally about her ambition to be an Air Hostess and about her longing to visit other countries and, of course, about her brother in England who was always writing to her, telling her about all the interesting things she would see if she had the chance to travel.

She returned to school to be told by the Headmistress that the School Certificate results had arrived and that she had passed with flying colours. She felt content. In a week's time, she had the longed-for letter, saying that the Airline had accepted her for training. She rushed along to show it to the Headmistress.

"Well done, Anna," she said. "Only four girls were chosen out of three thousand applications. Good luck to you, my dear," she added as she looked at the excited young girl standing in front of her.

Although Anna had felt all along that she would be accepted, when the truth was actually confirmed, hysterical tears and laughter welled up into her throat. She managed to control herself and said in a halting voice, "Oh, how wonderful! Thankyou."

The following week, she said 'goodbye' to her formal schooling forever, and once again found herself knocking on the Chief Training Officer's door.

Chapter 2

THE MOCK-UP

Anna looked round the classroom and noticed the photographs on the walls. How competent the stewards and stewardesses looked as they served the meals and drinks to the passengers! She felt the smooth, clean wood of her desk and sat back in the comfortably-shaped chair, looking at the models of various aircraft set up in front of the blackboard.

It was a new experience for Anna to be in a class with young men. Of the seventeen trainees, there were only five girls; they were certainly in the minority and she hoped they could hold their own, both intellectually and socially.

There was an expectant hush as the door opened and the Chief Training Officer, Tom Clinton, walked in. They all stood up.

"Sit down," he said. "You're not at school now. You needn't stand up when I come into the room, as long as you stop talking and listen to what I have to say!"

At that moment, the door opened again and Julia Symonds walked in. Tom turned and smiled at her.

"Now you all met Miss Symonds at your interview," he said. "She and I will be giving you most of your lectures; on catering, flying and standby duties, briefings etc.; but nurses, doctors, firemen, security officers and other people who work in different parts of the Airport will also come and tell you about their duties. You have eight weeks training on the ground before you start flying."

"I thought we started flying straight away and did all our training in the air," called out Simeon.

"You do some training in the planes, but it would be too bewildering for you to learn everything in the air, let alone the effect it would have on the passengers to have some one with no experience at all trying to serve them. They wouldn't think much of our Airline if we arranged things that way, would they?" There was a murmur of disappointed assent from the class.

"To remind you to take your work seriously," continued Tom, "at the end of each week there's an exam, which you're expected to pass. If you fail more than two exams, that's the end of your career with us!" He paused for a moment to let the words sink in. "Now Miss Symonds will have a word with you."

He stepped aside and nodded to Julia Symonds who was sitting near a large model of a Comet. She smiled at him and stood up.

"I've made arrangements for your accommodation," she said. "Boys at the 'Y.M.', girls at the 'Y.W.'; but if anyone wants to live with their family or friends, please let me know. However, before you decide, remember, you'll be called out at any time of the day or night, so unless the people you intend to live with don't mind being woken up at two o'clock in the morning, perhaps you'd better accept the accommodation I have arranged. Later on, when you're earning a lot more money, you can find a flat of your own. Now, have you any questions?"

"Please, when do we get our uniforms?" asked Asha.

"Actually, you'll each be given a second-hand uniform this afternoon," answered Julia Symonds. "Now, don't look upset," she continued, as she saw at least half a dozen faces drop. "They've all been cleaned and they're in perfect condition. The tailor will make them fit as if they were new. As soon as you've finished your three months' probation, you'll be given two brand new uniforms, made to measure, and these will be replaced as they wear out."

"Don't we go up in an aeroplane at all for two months?" asked Anna, feeling very disappointed.

"Yes, you do," answered Tom. "I've arranged for you to go up in a DC3 next week, so that you'll at least know what it feels like to be airborne. Have any of you been up at all?" he asked.

Simeon put up his hand. "I flew here from Uganda in a 'Friendship'," he volunteered.

"How did you like it?" asked Tom.

"I was very frightened and I felt funny inside," replied Simeon. "But I think I'll be all right next time!"

The trainees laughed.

"Has anyone else been up?" asked Julia.

There was no reply. None of the others had been near an aircraft. They had only seen them as tiny specks in the sky, where, to unpractised eyes, one silhouette looked much the same as another.

"A question please," said one of the girls timidly.

"Yes," said Julia, expectantly.

"Can an aircraft fly backwards?" asked the girl.

A roar of laughter echoed round the room. The girl crouched down in her chair, looking as if she wanted to sink through the floor. Tom and Julia exchanged a glance. "Was the girl trying to be funny? If so, she had better be squashed straight away," was the unspoken comment which passed between them.

Tom looked at the girl's appealing face and asked her name.

"Mary," she whispered in a tone that was hardly audible.

"Well, Mary, that's not such a silly question as it sounds," he said, "Cars, lorries, trains and ships, even helicopters can all go backwards as well as forwards, so why can't aeroplanes?"

The class stopped tittering and looked interested.

"As a matter of fact they can't," Tom continued. "Because they would lose so much speed in order to reverse that they couldn't possibly stay up in the sky. Luckily there's plenty of room in the air, and in the unlikely event of the pilot's taking a wrong turning, he could fly round until he reached the direction in which he should be going."

Anna noticed the grateful look on Mary's face. Not only had Tom Clinton stopped the class ridiculing her, but he had also imparted an interesting piece of knowledge in answer to her question.

"Why do some people call us 'Stewardesses' and others call us 'Air Hostesses'?" asked Anna.

Tom smiled. "When girls first started flying as cabin staff, they were all called 'Air Hostesses' and some Airlines still use this term; but you do the same work as the men and they are called 'stewards', so it seems more sensible to call you girls, 'stewardesses'. In our aircraft, above each passenger's seat, you'll see the words 'STEW BELL' — that's us! Boys or girls!" he answered.

"Thank you," said Anna.

"Now we'll go to the 'mock-up'," said Tom.

"Whatever's that?" exclaimed a dozen voices.

"You'll see," said Tom.

"I'll leave you in good hands while I go and work out my 'Duty Roster' for next week," said Julia.

Tom opened the door for her. "Not too many scrambled eggs," she said to him as she went out.

Anna sensed that this was some private joke they shared and a blinding flash of jealousy took her by surprise. It was over almost before she realized it had hit her and she followed Tom along the passage with the other trainees, feeling rather subdued.

About half way down, Tom threw open a door on the right. It looked like an ordinary door, opening into an ordinary office, but when they stepped inside they all gave gasps and exclamations of surprise. Instead of a room, they found themselves inside an exact replica of the cabin of an aeroplane.

There were sixteen seats, arranged in pairs on either side of a gangway. Safety belts were neatly placed in such a way that it appeared simple to fasten them without muddling up the straps. The window, by each seat, was in the shape of a large port-hole. At the back was a galley, or kitchen, complete with an electric cooker, two urns, storage space for food and trays, and a small, but immaculate, bar.

"Now, I want four volunteers to act as 'cabin staff'," said Tom. "The rest of you choose a seat, sit down and fasten the safety belts round your waist. Then just relax and make yourselves comfortable."

"Do the passengers have to wear these all the time they're in the air?" asked Anna, sitting down and struggling with the clasp of the safety belt.

"No," answered Tom. "Only when the pilot is taking-off and landing, and at certain other times when it's bumpy."

Simeon, Jean, Asha and John offered to be 'cabin staff' and Tom showed them how to fasten the safety belts correctly and told them to walk along the gangway and help the 'passengers'. Then he called them into the 'galley' and gave Simeon and Jean each a pencil and a sheet of paper and told them to ask each 'passenger' what he would like to drink.

"But," he said in a loud voice, "I'm afraid your drinks must be confined to lemon, orange, lime juice or 'coke'; the airline can't afford anything stronger!"

"However shall we remember who has asked for what?" said Asha.

"If you look on the back of each seat, you'll see a number," said Tom. "So it's simple. You just write down the number of the seat and beside it the drink that the passenger has ordered."

Ten minutes later, giggles and guffaws of merriment came from both the 'passengers' and 'cabin staff' as the drinks were handed round. Asha gave Anna a bottle and forgot to open it; John opened a bottle of orange soda and let it fizz out of the top and run all over the floor, narrowly missing someone's lap; Jean gave someone the wrong drink. Only Simeon, who had seen all this before, calmly unfastened the large press-stud which held the table in place in front of his 'passenger', and served him correctly, pouring the orange into a glass and handing it on a pink, plastic tray.

"Now we'll make some scrambled eggs," said Tom, an amused expression coming over his face.

Anna thought he was joking, but, sure enough, he produced about half a dozen eggs, some butter, milk, salt and pepper from a cupboard in the galley and switched on one of the electric hot plates.

"There's not enough room for everyone to see what I'm doing," said Tom. "The four of you in the back seats come and watch and the rest put up your tables and read through the booklets in the seat pockets. You'll all get a turn in the galley — we spend quite a lot of time practising in here."

The 'passengers' lifted up their tables and fixed them, with the large press stud, to the seat in front. In the wide pocket underneath, they found an attractive folder and inside there were maps of the routes along which the aircraft flew; pamphlets on 'safety-precautions', use of oxygen masks and putting on life-belts, notes on 'Bar Service' and a description of the aircraft.

Anna and three of the men went and stood beside Tom in the galley and watched him deftly break eggs into a basin and whisk them up with some salt and pepper. Meanwhile he put some butter to melt in a large saucepan and showed the trainees how to lay up the breakfast trays with plates, cups, cutlery, packets of salt, pepper and sugar, and a roll on each small plate. In no time at all, he was serving out scrambled eggs and telling the four 'stewards' to take the trays round to the 'passengers'.

"We'll make some coffee now and that'll do for our mid-morning snack," he said.

Anna noticed that he had already switched on one of the electric urns and the water was now bubbling merrily!

By this time, the trainees had all decided that working in the 'mock-up' was going to be good fun. Lunchtime came before they realised the morning had gone, and Tom walked over to the canteen beside Anna.

"How do you think you're going to enjoy the course?" he asked.

"I think it's wonderful so far," she answered, her eyes shining.

They walked on in silence for a while.

"Why are you so keen on scrambled eggs?" she asked on an impulse.

He laughed reminiscently. "Well, Miss Symonds and I were on our first night flight with three trainees. I was about to tell them to go and ask the First Class passengers what kind of eggs they wanted for breakfast, when we passed over an air pocket. The aircraft gave an unexpected lurch and I dropped a heavy frying pan on to the cartons of eggs which Miss Symonds had just put on the table near the cooker. Every single one broke! So we scooped them up and put them into a bowl. 'Scrambled eggs only on the menu today' said Miss Symonds. 'It's up to you to make the passengers think that's just what they ordered!' So after that, we decided it was most important to teach stewards and stewardesses how to make scrambled eggs!"

Anna laughed as she pictured their plight.

"Have you been in this country long?" she asked as they neared the canteen.

"I was here before you were born, " Tom replied. "My father came over when I was about nine and I went to school here. Then the War started and my parents went to England. I finished my schooling there and went straight into the Air Force. I trained as a pilot and flew 'fighters'. After a year I was shot down and taken prisoner. When the War was over, I went to University, but I longed to go back to flying, so I applied to one of the big Airlines."

"And what happened?" asked Anna, as Tom paused and a bitter expression passed over his face.

"When I landed after being shot down, I must have hit my head," continued Tom. "I remember having blinding headaches for weeks and weeks, gradually they lessened and after some time, disappeared but the blow must have affected a nerve in my brain; that in turn, affected my eyesight. I passed the pilot's interview, but failed the sight test."

"And then?" said Anna softly.

"Oh, I was very upset at the time," Tom went on. "I wandered round the country, taking one job after another — any old thing that came along. Then one day, I had a letter from a friend who was a navigator with this Airline. He knew my history and simply said there was a job going as Chief Air Steward, mainly to be in charge of training, and suggested I should apply for it. I thought about it for a while and felt the longing to fly again. So I applied, was accepted — and, well, here I am." He finished with a smile.

"I suppose you've flown all over Africa," said Anna. "You must know my country better than I know it myself."

"Yes," answered Tom. "I know it pretty well. And I love it," he added, half under his breath.

Chapter 3

FIRST TIME UP

Anna found it difficult to sleep, she was so excited. Tom had told the trainees that he had arranged for them to go up on a flight the following day. At the first sign of the sunrise, Anna got up and dressed. She did not feel like eating any breakfast, but forced down a cup of tea and some bread and butter. At 9 o'clock, they all assembled on the tarmac, excited, but nervous.

"We'll just go and take a look at some of the aircraft before we go up," said Tom.

The seventeen trainees followed him over to the nearest plane. It was smaller than some, but Anna felt like a tiny speck as she stood near it.

"That's like the one I went on," said Simeon, in a slightly superior tone.

"See if you can tell us something about it, then," said Tom. "What's its name? How many people can it take? Tell us anything you can remember."

"It's called a 'Friendship'," began Simeon. "I can remember counting eleven rows of seats, two on each side of the gangway, so it can take forty-four passengers. I don't know how many there were in the crew."

"On a 'Friendship' there's always a pilot, (he's called the Captain); the co-pilot, (he's the First Officer); and often there's a navigator or engineer as well. If there are only two in the crew, then the First Officer also becomes the navigator and engineer! Do you remember how many 'cabin staff' there were?" asked Tom.

"There was one steward and one stewardess, as far as I can remember," answered Simeon. "The steward was in charge," he added, looking hard at the girls.

"Yes, there are two cabin staff working on the Friendship," replied Tom. "But the men aren't always in charge; it depends on how long they've been flying. You'll probably start on Friendships, but at first you'll be 'supernumerary', that's to say you'll be an 'extra', besides the usual two. You'll be told what to do, so you can get some practice without having the full responsibility of thinking of everything yourself."

They walked over to a larger aircraft.

"This one's called a 'Comet'," said Tom. "It takes seventy-five passengers and four cabin staff. It was the first pure jet aircraft; I mean the first plane to fly without any propellers. From here, they fly westwards to Rome, Paris, London; and eastwards to Aden, Karachi, Bombay. You'll all be flying in these eventually."

They stood gazing at the huge, beautiful streamlined machine and Anna was just going to ask if they could go inside, when Tom said, "Now we'll go and take a look at one of the largest aircraft in the world!"

They walked over to where an enormous aeroplane was standing on the tarmac. Anna felt smaller and more insignificant than ever.

"It's colossal!" she whispered in awe.

"It certainly is," said Tom. "Do you know, it's as high as a three-storeyed house and you could play a game of cricket on each wing! It weighs a hundred and sixty-two tons, that's about as much as a hundred and fifty cars," he added, emphasizing how enormous this bird of the air really was.

"Which airlines fly these?" asked Anna, her eyes shining with excitement, as she contemplated the immensity of the machine and wondered how it could possibly get up into the air, let alone stay there!"

"Several airlines already have them," answered Tom. He paused for a moment. "I'll let you into a secret," he continued in a low voice. "Our airline has three on order and the first one is to be delivered next week."

He noticed Anna, gazing starry-eyed at the VC 10.

"One day you might graduate to serving in one of these," he said to her. "But first you must prove your worth on the smaller planes."

"Once someone told me that these aircraft had an emergency plane built in the tail," said Anna, laughing. "The end does look rather like a small plane. I can see what they mean now."

The trainees roared with laughter. Tom looked at Anna and smiled. A look of shared amusement and understanding passed between them.

"Why have all these aircraft got numbers or letters on them?" asked Mary.

"Those are their 'registration numbers'," said Tom. "They all have numbers, like motor cars, so that anyone can tell at a glance where a plane belongs.

"Look at the 'G' on this VC 10 — that shows it's from Britain; that Boeing over there," (he pointed to another large plane, but one of a different shape), "that has a 'VH' on it, which shows it's from Australia; the one near it has '4X' on it; that's from Israel."

"They've got other numbers and figures as well," observed John.

"Those are their 'code numbers'," explained Tom. "The pilot uses these when he talks to the Officer in the Control Tower, asking permission to land, for example. The Officer uses this number when he is giving the pilot instructions; in this way, there can be no possible mistake as to which aircraft he is calling in."

"It must take ages to learn all the numbers and codes," said Anna.

"You'll find you soon get to know them by seeing them often," replied Tom. "Now, it's time for our flight. Follow me!"

They walked after Tom to what appeared to be a very small aircraft indeed after the huge VC 10.

"This is a DC 3, or Dakota aircraft," explained Tom. "We only do short flights in these and as there is only one person on duty in the cabin, you can be kept pretty busy. Come and meet your pilot."

The pilot, tall and confident, walked across to the group, the First Officer by his side.

"Morning all," he said to the students. "Where do you want to go?"

No one answered.

"Well, we'll do a few 'loops' over the airport shall we, and 'buzz' a few buildings in the town!" he said with a perfectly straight face.

Anna looked up, alarmed, and saw the First Officer and Tom exchange glances and nod at the serious-looking students. Then they both burst out laughing when they saw their worried faces.

"That's how people say pilots talk and act," said Tom. "They say they take every opportunity to perform stunts, and spend the rest of the time playing cards and joking with the passengers; whereas, in reality, there could hardly be any group of people who take their work more seriously."

"Yes," said the pilot with a grin. "We even keep an eye on 'George' when he's flying the plane."

"George!" exclaimed John in surprise. "Is he an extra member of the crew?"

"In a way, yes," answered the pilot. "George always comes up to give us a rest. He's been with us now since the early 1940's. He's actually the 'automatic pilot'."

The students looked puzzled.

"You see, in every country in the world, there are a series of radio beacons; the pilot sets the course and flies the plane along the route to its destination, guided by these beacons. 'George' is set to a certain wavelength and he can follow the course by himself. When he's flying, the pilot can relax a little and perhaps take a walk along the gangway and have a chat with the cabin staff and passengers. Of course, we don't trust 'George' entirely; one of us always watches him to see that he keeps on course."

The students looked relieved at this explanation.

"All right," said the pilot to Tom. "Let them all pile aboard."

Then he heaved himself up into the cockpit and started checking the instruments.

"In you all get," said Tom, indicating the open passenger door. The students looked at each other.

"Follow me then," said Tom. "Ladies first!" he added, smiling at the girls.

Then he walked up the steps and waited at the top. Anna skipped up after him, followed by Jean, Asha and Mary. Then came the boys, headed by gimeon and John.

"Mind your heads," said Tom. "Bend down as you go through the hatch. Sit down anywhere," he said, seeing a group standing awkwardly near the door, blocking up the gangway. "Then strap the safety belt round your waist and get ready for take-off."

The trainees each found a seat and relaxed back in comfort. Tom walked down the gangway, handing out sweets and making sure they had fastened their belts properly, before sitting down at the back in the single seat reserved for the steward.

The engines revved up and Anna felt her ears resound with the noise. The propellers whirled round; the chocks were removed and the machine cruised down the runway, slowly at first, then faster and faster until Anna felt she was being drawn back in her seat. She was conscious of a peculiar pain in her ears and she felt they were bulging outwards, muffling the sound of the roaring engines.

"Suck your sweets and swallow hard," came Tom's voice over the 'Public Address System'.

Anna swallowed hard and felt a 'popping' sensation in her ears. She looked down and saw the well-oiled under-carriage fold up and disappear effortlessly into the flaps, which closed like the snap of a crocodile's jaws round its reluctant victim.

The plane rose up through the thick layer of cloud and into the sky above. To Anna, it appeared, at first, as if they were upside down, with the sky as blue as the sea, and the heavy clouds beneath, but after a time she thought the clouds looked like a huge snow-field, solid enough to sit on and slide back down to the earth.

When the plane straightened out at about 16,000 feet, Anna realized that the 'popping' sensation in her ears had vanished and they no longer felt congested. In fact, she felt quite normal!

The clouds cleared and Anna looked down to the earth and saw her Geography lessons come to life. There was a relief map spread out before her; the rivers meandering along their winding course on their long journey towards the sea; the red earth roads, belying their ruts and corrugations, looked like smooth, coloured ribbons, scarring the green of the fields. Then Anna noticed the little thatched huts, looking like toys amongst the banana groves and tiny fields of maize; cattle seemed no larger than the tiny plastic replicas of animals she had seen in the city shops; people were smaller than dolls.

As they turned to fly back over the city, Anna could see the shadow of the aircraft on the earth beneath and marvelled that the machine could keep up in the sky. She caught a glimpse of the symmetrical rows of houses, as the plane started to lose height, and suddenly they were surrounded by a thick grey mist. She felt a sick, dragging sensation in her stomach and she hoped she was not going to be ill.

She felt weightless and dizzy and there was that congested feeling again in her ears as the pilot flew lower. Exclamations of "Oh!" and "Help!" came from the passengers as the plane hit an air pocket. Anna felt as if she was going down in a lift very quickly indeed, and then, as if some one had pressed a button impatiently, they came up again with a jerk.

The plane swooped down and turned sideways, one wing much lower than the other. Anna saw the earth coming up to meet them as they veered round at a crazy angle. They flew low over the town and saw the roads, the cars, the shops; Parliament Buildings and the Clock Tower reaching up to the sky; tiny people, like ants seething along the pavements. Then the buildings were left behind and Anna was quite sure they were going to land in the Game Park. Having survived a perilous trip into 'space', they would now be eaten by lions, hyenas and jackals, their remains finished off by vultures. She shuddered! But all was well! She felt the slight bump as the wheels touched down on the tarmac runway and heard the changed note of the engines as they strained against the curbing brake in the pilot's capable hands.

None of the trainees were really sorry when their first flight came to an end. The plane taxied towards the Terminal Buildings and the pilot brought it to a smooth halt. Tom opened the door and fixed the head-pad in position as the steps were wheeled up.

"Out you get!" he said to the rather bewildered passengers. "Next time it won't feel nearly so strange."

They were all curiously exhausted after their experience and were glad to return to the firm ground of the classroom. Julia was waiting to give them a talk on 'stand-by' duties, but when she saw the group, she decided to let them go home and rest. The lecture could wait until the following day.

Chapter 4

OVER THE SADDLE OF KILIMANJARO

At last Anna was to go on her first flight as a fully-fledged stewardess. Mary was to go with her, and Tom was coming along to be in charge and tell them what to do. It was the Coastal Flight, on a 'Friendship', travelling to Dar-es-Salaam with several stops in between.

About half-an-hour before the plane was due to leave, Anna, Mary and Tom were in the cabin, checking the amount of drinks and refreshments and making sure there were clean towels, soap and hand lotion in the toilets.

"You see that the safety belts are laid across the seats correctly," said Tom to Mary. "And at the same time, check that a folder is in each seat pocket, complete with all the maps and pamphlets — and don't forget the 'airsick bags'," he added as Mary walked off down the gangway.

Then Tom handed Anna three silver trays and a bag of sweets and told her to fill up the trays and also to put a few small packets of cotton-wool on one side.

"Some passengers get a slight ear-ache during take-off and landing and they like to put cotton wool in their ears, but you won't find many people want it," he explained.

Tom checked the amount of sandwiches, fruit and cakes to be served en route and then he told Anna to fill up and switch on the electric urns so as to be ready to make tea and coffee soon after take-off.

The pilot opened the door between the flight deck and the cabin, and strolled along to the galley.

"Hallo," he said, when he saw Anna and Mary. "So we've two new stewardesses on board, have we? What's your name?" he asked Anna, who was standing near him. "And can you make good coffee?"

"My name's Anna and I'm not so sure about the coffee!" she replied.

"Well, I'll have Bovril then," answered the pilot and he disappeared through the doorway, back into the crew's compartment, Anna heard him and his co-pilot and navigator make the numerous necessary checks before starting up the engines.

"The passengers are coming," said Tom. "Anna, you stand just inside the doorway, ready to welcome them aboard. And Mary, you go a little way down the gangway and help them choose their seats and fasten their safety belts. Afterwards, Mary and I will hand round the sweets."

I thought all the passengers had numbers on their tickets," said Anna.

"Not on these local flights," said Tom. "They just sit where they like."

Anna smiled at the passengers and said 'good afternoon' to each one as they passed, and soon Mary had helped them to settle comfortably in their seats, stowing their hand luggage underneath.

The propellers started, at first slowly, then faster and faster until a yellow ring about twelve feet in diameter was all that could be seen of the huge blades. Anna felt the expectant thrill as the plane sped faster and faster along the runway, and without looking down she could feel the exact moment when they left the ground.

"You may unfasten your seat belts and smoke if you wish," came Tom's voice over the 'Public Address System'.

Anna saw Mary get up from her seat beside a personable middle-aged business-man; she thought she had rather a nerve, but then she remembered that stewardesses were allowed to sit next to the passengers at take off and landing, and even during the flight, provided they had a slack moment and did not stay too long with one person.

As soon as they had unfastened their seat belts, Anna and Mary each took a pencil and paper and asked the passengers what they would like to drink — tea, coffee, cold drinks or something alcoholic. Then they prepared the trays and handed round the sandwiches with the passengers' requests. The service was brisk and efficient and in a few minutes, everyone had been given what he wanted.

Anna carried a cup of Bovril on a tray to the pilot.

"Enjoying the trip?" he asked, as he took the tray from her.

"Oh, yes," said Anna enthusiastically.

"Take a look from here then," he said. "George is flying, so you needn't do anything with the controls."

He got up and beckoned Anna to sit in his seat.

"I'll leave you in charge and while my drink's getting cool I'll go and stretch my legs," he said, and winked at his co-pilot and navigator.

"Don't worry, chaps, Anna will drive!" He pushed back the sliding door and closed it behind him.

"Don't mind us!" said the First Officer.

Anna sat down in the pilot's seat and gazed in wonder at the mass of instruments on the huge panel in front of her.

"However does he manage to read all these things at the same time?" she said, half to herself. "And whatever are they all?"

"Oh, it becomes quite automatic when you've flown long enough," said the First Officer. "It's like driving a car — you know instinctively if anything is even slightly off normal."

"But there are so many more instruments to look at than in a car," said Anna.

"Yes," agreed the First Officer. "You're right there. Often when I'm driving a car over the hills and the mist comes down, I wish I had some of these instruments, telling me the weather ahead and any immovable objects I might encounter."

Anna looked down for a moment through the wisps of cloud and saw a winding river twisting, snake-like, across the countryside.

"It really is just like a map come to life," she said. "I don't think I'll ever get used to flying. Are you used to it? Do you take it all for granted?" she asked.

"We take the job for granted," said the voice of the pilot, who had returned while Anna was contemplating the wonders of the earth beneath.

"But we're always conscious of the responsibility we have towards those who fly with us, aren't we, Bill?" he said to the First Officer.

"Yes, that's true enough," replied Bill. "Most of us like people and find we get along with them easily, so we laugh and joke a great deal and many people think we haven't a care in the world!"

He let out a deep sigh, but as Anna looked at him, his mouth stretched into a huge grin.

"I don't think it'll make us old before our time, you know!" said the pilot. "Go back now, Anna. 'Stew Bell's' ringing and Mary is brewing some more coffee. She's wondering if you've jumped overboard!"

Anna got up to go when the pilot called her back.

"I don't like milk in my Bovril," he said. "*You* have it and see what it tastes like."

Anna took the cup and drank the light brown liquid. She did not think there was much wrong with it, but she said nothing and went to prepare some more, remembering she had been told to use only water with these soup-like drinks.

Tom and Mary were in the galley and she whispered to them what she had done.

Mary giggled. "That's not as bad as me the other day," she said. "I put some orange soda in a passenger's whisky! He *was* cross!"

Anna took the freshly-prepared Bovril to the pilot.

"That's better — thanks!" he grinned.

When she returned to the galley, she saw one of the lights flashing. Quickly, she walked along the rows of seats to see who was ringing. It was number seven, seat B — the aisle seat, seven rows from the front.

"Yes, Madam," said Anna, pulling down the bell to cancel the call.

"I feel a bit funny," said an elderly lady. "I've never flown before. Can you give me anything?"

"I'll fetch you a pill and a glass of water," said Anna. "Another time, if you're travelling by air, I should ask your doctor or chemist for something to take before you start the journey; then you'll feel perfectly all right."

"Thanks, dear," said the woman as Anna thrust an open 'air-sick' bag into her hands just in time.

"You'll feel a lot better now, Madam," she said. "I'll fetch the pill and some water. How far are you travelling?"

"Only to Moshi," whispered the old lady. "I'm a bit nervous, really; that's the trouble with me, I think."

Anna took the soiled bag and handed the old lady a fresh one. Then she quietly brought her a glass of water and an 'air-sick' tablet. She sprinkled some refreshing lavender water on to a small towel and gently wiped the old lady's face. Then she gave her another perfumed towel for her hands.

"That's better. Thanks, dear," said the old lady, and handed Anna the empty glass. "I'll be all right now, knowing you're looking after me so well."

Anna left the old lady and as she walked back to the galley, another passenger called her and asked for a drink. She went to fetch it and as she was returning, she happened to glance out of the window. The sight that met her eyes made her catch her breath and stand still. Out of the clouds rose the 'sugar-cake' peak of Kilimanjaro. The plane flew so near that she had a burning desire to break the window and feel the white, ethereal substance which covered the top. She had never seen a mountain at such close quarters and gazed enraptured as they flew nearer. She noticed how the 'snow-line' stopped abruptly and age-old clefts in the rock ran down from underneath, carved out long ago by burning lava. This had shot out of the vast crater, gouging deep runnels and fighting a losing battle in a vain attempt to conquer the hissing snow.

"Look this side!" exclaimed the excited voice of one of the passengers.

Momentarily forgetting her duties, Anna put down her tray on an empty seat and swiftly took a step over to the opposite side of the plane. She gasped as she saw the clear, cruel beauty of the ragged rocks rising out of the flat layer of cloud. They were flying over the saddle of, Kilimanjaro, between the twin peaks of Africa's highest mountain.

The intense white of the snow and the ice-cold, clear blue sky gave Anna a strange feeling and although she knew they were travelling at a speed of about three hundred miles an hour, she felt as if they were hovering by the side of the crater, still, unmoving. She looked away from the window and found Tom gazing at her intently.

"It's good to share such an experience," he said quietly, understanding the intensity of the moment.

His deep blue eyes looked into her brown ones and she felt as she had done on the day he had come to speak to the school, and again when she arrived to commence her training. Time stood still as Anna returned his look. No words were spoken as she tore herself away and gathered up the remaining threads of her duties.

"We are now landing at Moshi Airport," said Mary's voice

over the Public Address System. "We hope those passengers now leaving us have had a pleasant flight and we shall have the pleasure of flying with you again. We shall be stopping here for twenty minutes; those in transit may remain on board but must not smoke or use the toilets whilst the aircraft is on the ground. Please remain seated until the aircraft has come to a complete standstill."

Anna stood at the top of the steps and helped the passengers down, saying 'good-bye' to those who were disembarking; watching those 'in transit' receive their blue cards from the Ground Stewardess at the bottom of the steps.

"Come on, you two, just time for a fresh lime juice," said Tom. "There's nothing more refreshing." Mary and Anna agreed and walked quickly after Tom as the cleaners ran up the steps with brushes and cloths, ready to clean up the almost spotless cabin. As Anna walked across the short width of tarmac, she looked back, fascinated, as the petrol tanker was wheeled into position and the fire-men stood to attention beside their machine. She noticed the yellow chocks under the wheels and saw one of the ground staff check the amount of petrol being put in and heard a voice calling out the weight of the on-coming luggage.

"Come on!" called Tom. "Stop standing there as if you hadn't seen it all before."

"Well, I haven't," replied Anna, with spirit, tearing herself away and following him into the lounge. "There's always something new happening anyway."

"Not really," said Tom. "It's just that you haven't taken in all that's involved in the routine of flying and how many people are needed to keep the time schedules running smoothly."

A quick drink and it was time for them to return to the aircraft. They ran up the steps and quickly walked down the gangway, picking up the cushions and placing the safety belts crossed tidily on the seats; putting the magazines and pamphlets in the racks and filling up the silver trays with sweets. They had just finished when the passengers came on board.

"Anna, you welcome the passengers on board this time," said Tom.

Anna sat down on the steward's seat and nervously picked up the 'intercom' and started speaking.

"We welcome you on board, ladies and gentlemen..."

"You're supposed to be welcoming the passengers, not us," said a voice. "There are no ladies amongst the crew anyway!"

Embarrassed, Anna realized that she had not switched the controls to the 'P.A. System', but was still connected to the crew's cabin!

She switched over and started again. "Ladies and Gentlemen," she began. Her voice wavered and sounded about three pitches higher than usual. She looked up at Tom for encouragement, but he was busy preparing some coffee and not looking in her direction. She took a breath and went on.

"We welcome you aboard this aircraft. Refreshments will be served soon after take-off. Our flight to Mombasa will take fifty-five minutes and we shall be flying at a height of 16,000 feet. Please fasten your seat belts ready for take-off, and kindly refrain from smoking until we are in the air. We hope you have a pleasant flight. Thank you."

Anna heaved a great sigh and felt herself shaking all over as she replaced the receiver on its hook.

"Well done," whispered Mary, who had come up beside her. Anna fastened her seat belt and Mary and Tom sat down amongst the passengers.

"Tanga, Zanzibar, Dar-es-Salaam," thought Anna. "It's like a bus; no sooner are we up than we start coming down again!"

The plane rose quickly and then straightened out.

"Go on," said Tom in a loud whisper. He had unfastened his safety belt and was leaning towards her.

For a moment, Anna's mind went blank and she could not think what he meant. He nodded towards the sign up front where the illuminated notice had been switched off.

"Oh," breathed Anna, and picked up the receiver once more.

"You may unfasten your safety belts and smoke if you wish," she said, and this time her voice sounded more normal, although she found her hand was still shaking as she replaced the instrument in its holder.

"Trays, quickly," said Mary, and they were soon walking swiftly down the gangway, handing out sandwiches, cakes and biscuits, while Tom followed with a large teapot.

It was 9 o'clock by the time they reached Dar; and it was 10 o'clock by the time the transport had dropped Anna and Mary at the door of the hostel where they were to stay the night.

"Sleep well, girls," called Tom as the coach drove away. "I'll call for you at 9 o'clock tomorrow morning and we'll go and have a swim. Our flight doesn't leave until four o'clock in the afternoon."

It was sticky and hot after Nairobi, but Anna and Mary were so tired that they slept soundly. They awoke early, feeling refreshed and looking forward to a few hours relaxing by the sea.

Chapter 5

AWKWARD PASSENGERS

Punctually at nine o'clock, Tom called at the hostel. Anna and Mary were just finishing their breakfast and hurriedly gulped down their third cup of coffee.

"We've about three hours if you come now," said Tom. "I've brought a picnic lunch so we needn't come back until it's time to change into uniform and go to the airport."

"Where are we going?" asked Mary.

"We're going to a lovely little place called 'Oyster Bay'," said Tom. "We're meeting the crew there. It's a wonderful spot; calm water; soft white ; sand and palm trees. There's a hotel where you can change into your costumes."

He felt a peculiar silence and glanced up and saw Anna and Mary looking at one another.

"What's the matter?" he asked. "Don't you want to come?"

"We... we...," began Anna.

"We haven't got any costumes," blurted out Anna and Mary together.

Tom laughed. "No wonder you were worried," he said. "Haven't you been to the sea before?"

"We didn't like to tell you," said Anna, looking downcast.

"But why not? It's wonderful showing people something

new. I'll tell you what we'll do; we'll go into town first and you can buy yourselves a swimming-costume apiece. You'll be needing them a lot in your chosen career, so you might as well get them now."

He drove them into town and stopped outside one of the large stores.

"Don't be too long," he called out.

Anna and Mary wandered round until an assistant asked them what they wanted. She showed them dozens of bathing-costumes of different patterns, styles and colours. Eventually, Anna chose a yellow one and Mary, a pale blue one. They tried them on in a little room at the back of the shop and the assistant came and said they looked very nice. Between them, they had just enough money to pay for the costumes and two gaily-coloured beach towels. Tom was waiting patiently in the car park opposite the store and within half an hour they were at Oyster Bay.

The pilot and the rest of the crew were lazing on the sand when they arrived. Anna and Mary felt rather self-conscious when they changed into their bathing-suits, but when they saw other girls lying on the sand, dressed even more scantily, they soon got used to the idea! They splashed in the sea and lay under the shade of the palm trees, drinking cool, fresh lime juice and nibbling sausage rolls, chicken sandwiches and coconuts.

Anna watched the white foam rising, falling, receding, advancing, until her eyes closed and she began to doze off.

"One more dip and then we must go — paradise for us is short-lived," said Tom and he shook Anna gently until she

40

awoke and then they all raced down to the water. Anna and Mary sat on the edge and let the waves break over them as they watched the men swim strongly out to a raft anchored a hundred yards or so from the shore.

"Not a bad life," said the pilot, when they returned.

They stood for a moment, their wet, bronzed bodies glistening in the sun.

"Change now and back we go," said Tom.

When they arrived at the airport, they were told that the plane was delayed. The passengers arrived, checked in and waited. Five minutes before they should have been called, the plane had still not arrived. A voice over the loud speaker apologized and told them that the plane had been delayed and would arrive shortly.

"Go and hand round some free refreshment chits," said Tom. "That will keep them happy for a while."

Anna and Mary walked round the lounge and found most of the passengers far from happy.

"What's the trouble?" asked an irate businessman. "I could have used the time in town. Why didn't you inform us we'd be late starting? What do you think I can do here?"

"I'm sorry, Sir," said Anna. "I'm afraid there's a delay."

"Delay! Of course there's a delay or we shouldn't be here," shouted the man unkindly. "Now my time's being wasted. WASTED!" he repeated, thumping his fist on the table so that the cups rattled and Anna jumped.

"I'm very sorry, Sir," she said, feeling it was all her fault.

"My husband will be waiting for me," complained an elderly

woman to Mary. "He doesn't like waiting around at airports. Do you think they've told him we won't be on time?"

"He'll be informed at the airport," said Mary, feeling utterly miserable.

"We spend more time waiting for the plane than it takes to fly from one place to another," said a young man to whom Anna handed the next refreshment chit.

By this time, Anna was nearly in tears. "I'm sorry, Sir," was all she could think of saying.

There was a faint sound in the distance and a speck in the sky grew larger and the noise was deafening as a huge aircraft dropped on to the runway and taxied towards the terminal.

The passengers in the lounge stood up as if they had been given an order, but the announcement over the loud speaker told them that it was not their flight. The plane was from overseas and flying to another destination. They sank back disconsolately as the crowd from the incoming plane surged noisily into the lounge.

At last there was an announcement that the long-awaited plane from Nairobi would be arriving in half an hour. There had been a slight fault in one of the cockpit instruments; the mechanic had taken an hour to locate the trouble and another hour to mend and test the instrument. "We are extremely sorry for the inconvenience and delay caused to our passengers," ended the voice over the loud speaker.

Sounds of 'I should think so too' emanated from the passengers, who were now more relieved than angry.

With a terrific roar, the engines of the overseas Boeing

started up and, as Anna watched, the powerful jets sent waves of vapour across the coconut plantation at the edge of the airfield, making the tall palms appear to shimmer and shake in a crazy, primitive dance; the hot air was forced backwards towards a row of flags near the terminal buildings, causing them to spring to life as if welcoming the passengers aboard.

Soon afterwards, the 'Friendship' arrived from Nairobi and within twenty minutes, it had re-fuelled; the incoming cabin staff and crew had exchanged a few words with those taking over; and the impatient passengers were ushered on board.

Tom was just about to tell the passengers that they could 'unfasten their seat belts and smoke if they wished', when there was a long, imperious ring and a red light showed on the switch-board in front of Anna. She jumped up and went along to see who was ringing. It was a young man on his first trip; he worked for a large business firm and was travelling to attend a conference. He smiled to himself as Anna came towards him.

"This is a pleasant way to travel," he thought. "Pretty girls at my beck and call!"

"What can I get for you, Sir?" asked Anna.

"I'll have a drink," said the young man. "Bring me the wine tariff please."

Anna disappeared once more and quickly returned with the 'Bar Service' card. The young man pretended to study it carefully.

"A double brandy and ginger, please," he said, after a few moments.

Anna went along to the bar and poured out a double tot of brandy and put it on a tray with a bottle of ginger.

"Thanks a lot," drawled the young man.

He wanted to talk to Anna, but she disappeared into the galley.

He looked above his head and pressed the 'Stew Call' button again. Within a moment, there was Anna, standing beside him once more. He felt like Aladdin with the magic lamp.

"What else can I get you, Sir?" she asked politely.

"Just sit down and talk to me," he replied, indicating the empty seat beside him.

"I'm very sorry, Sir, but I've got to help prepare the refreshments now," she said.

"Well, come back later — I'll reward you well for your services," said the young man, looking at her in a peculiar way.

Embarrassed beyond words, Anna turned and walked quickly back to the galley.

"What shall I do if that man keeps on ringing?" she asked Tom. "He's a one, really he is!"

"Just be polite — the passenger's always right!" chanted Tom, laughing.

In a few minutes the bell rang again.

"I'll go," said Tom.

Anna never knew exactly what Tom said to the young man, but he did not ring his bell again for the rest of the journey and when he left the plane he smiled at her and said he had had a very pleasant flight.

"There's ways and ways of telling the passenger he's right," said Tom, when Anna asked him what he had said to the young man!

Anna, Mary and Tom were having a quick cup of tea in the lounge while they were waiting for the plane to refuel, when the Ground Stewardess came up to them, dragging a reluctant, tearful little girl about ten years old.

"This is Sarah," she said. "Her mother brought her but when the plane was delayed, she had to leave her with me and get back to her other children. Sarah is going to school in Nairobi and this waiting around has upset her."

"I don't want to go to school! I don't want to go to school!" wailed the child. "All the others are staying at home; why should I be sent away?"

"I'll look after her," said Anna, glad of the responsibility.

"Let me bring you an orange soda," she said and went to fetch one, motioning to the Ground Stewardess to leave.

The child quietened, rubbed her tear-stained face and gave Anna a wet handshake. She accepted the orange and drank it through a straw with great tearful gulps.

"I want to go to the toilet, please, before the plane leaves," said the child meekly after a few moments.

Anna got up and accompanied her. She waited by the wash-basins.

When five minutes had passed, she began to get worried.

"Are you all right?" she called out. "It's nearly time for take-off."

And, indeed, she knew that by now she ought to be in the plane with Tom and Mary giving it a final tidy-up and inspection.

"I'm just coming," called Sarah.

Another few minutes elapsed.

"Please come now," said Anna. "I'm supposed to go on board before all the pasengers arrive; you can come with me if you like," she added as a final incentive. There was no reply.

Anna called again and rattled the door. In desperation she found a coin in her handbag and put it in the slot. She opened the door. There was no one inside. A small piece of torn red material hung in a strip over the hook of the window-sill.

Anna rushed back to the lounge. The passengers were being called to proceed to the aircraft. Tom and Mary had gone on ahead. She rushed through the door marked 'Crew Only', raced across to the aircraft and almost fell inside.

"The child's gone" she shouted. "She's climbed out through the lavatory window and run away!"

"Why ever didn't you go after her?" asked Tom.

"I didn't know she'd gone until it was too late!" replied Anna, fear and anxiety making her voice tremble.

"You and Mary welcome the passengers aboard," said Tom urgently. "And tell the pilot to hang on for a few minutes — no, don't you come," he said to Anna who was following him down the steps.

Out of one of the windows of the plane, he had caught a glimpse of a small figure flitting amongst the coconut palms beyond the airport boundary. He raced towards it and there ensued a rapid game of 'Hide and Seek' amongst the trees. The child was nimble on her feet, but doubling back on her tracks when she saw Tom pursuing her, she tripped over a fallen coconut and lay sobbing on a bed of leaves. Tom picked her up and popped a sweet into her mouth.

"It would have been a bit lonely out there in the dark, Sarah," he said. "You might not have been found till morning."

The child nestled against him and let him carry her, unresisting, to the plane.

"Wouldn't you like to walk up the steps by yourself?" he said.

Sarah nodded without speaking. He put her down and together they climbed up the steps.

"Oh good, you're just in time," said Anna, greeting her as if nothing had happened. "Let me see if you can fasten your safety belt yourself."

She led Sarah to an empty seat and gave her the straps.

"As soon as we're up, I'll bring you some comics and a jigsaw puzzle, or would you rather have some paper and crayons?"

"Some paper and crayons, please," said Sarah. "Then I can draw me running away! And, I say, we do get some food, don't we?"

Anna laughed happily, glad the child showed she liked her. "I'll bring you some sandwiches in just a few moments," she replied.

The flight was uneventful and when they arrived at Nairobi Airport, Sarah's aunt greeted a smiling, cheerful little girl, who immediately started telling her how much she had enjoyed the flight.

Anna was just breathing a sigh of relief that all was well, when there was a piercing scream from the lounge. With all the excitement of losing and recovering Sarah, Tom had forgotten to tell Anna that there was a chimpanzee on board. Instead of stopping in Nairobi, they were to fly on to Entebbe and deliver him to the zoo. This would be less of an upheaval for him than to be unloaded for the night and flown on the next day.

But Judo, the Chimp, had obviously thought he had been forgotten, and while his keeper had gone to the lounge for a cup of coffee, he had somehow managed to force open his crate. Now, with a great leap, he bounded through the doorway of the lounge and jumped on the refreshment counter. He snatched a bottle of 'coke' from a startled attendant and poured it into his mouth, spilling some of the bubbling liquid down the matted hair on his chest. He pushed open the door leading into the kitchen. Yells and screams followed as the staff rushed out, chased by Judo. His mouth was crammed full of sandwiches and cakes, a banana was sticking up in a ridiculous fashion behind each ear, making him look like a hairy devil!

Passengers scattered in all directions as Judo bounded back through the lounge, snatching a newspaper from a startled old man as he went. Tom, Anna, the keeper and some of the crew and passengers joined in the chase as Judo leapt up the steps of an aircraft that was just leaving for Europe. Passengers inside screamed helplessly, as they sat strapped in by their seat belts, too astounded, or paralyzed with fear, to press the release catch and run outside.

As a final fling, Judo picked up a man's briefcase, jumped out of the aircraft, narrowly escaping the arms of his keeper, and raced towards a hangar where a mechanic was lying on the ground inspecting the landing wheels of a large aircraft. Seeing the dark, cavernous hiding-place that housed the retractible undercarriage, Judo jumped in between the the flaps and lay peering out like a grotesque creature from outer space.

With great presence of mind, the mechanic ran outside and closed the doors of the hangar. The keeper rushed up breathlessly and cautiously let himself inside. Judo had had his fun; he let his keeper take hold of his collar and allowed himself to be led, captive, back to his crate, which was then nailed up very securely indeed!

Anna gave a sigh of relief when the aircraft took off again for its last leg that evening. As she fastened her seat belt, she looked out of the window and watched the sun drop lower and lower behind the trees. As the plane rose, a brilliant orange lit up the sky, making the hills look as if they would disappear at any moment in a great and terrible conflagration. Then all at once the edge of the earth melted into the horizon and a myriad stars appeared against the black backdrop of the sky.

For the next half hour, Anna was busy serving out drinks and refreshments, but when she had finished, she glanced once more out of the window. This time the twinkling lights of earth came into view, making her think of her family gathered round the fire in the little mud hut where she had been born.

"What a lot I shall have to tell them when I go on leave," she thought.

Chapter 6

OVERSEAS AT LAST

After about eight months, Anna and Mary were tired of living at the 'Y'; the set meals at specified times, the niggling notices of do's and don'ts; they were even tired of kind Miss Wangi, probably because she took such an interest in their comings and goings. So they decided to find a flat and set up housekeeping on their own.

It was not easy. They answered advertisements and seemed to spend most of their spare time in Estate Agents' Offices. The flats that were offered were either too large, or too small, or too expensive. At last, when they had almost given up trying, through a friend of a friend of Mary's, who knew a landlord, they found a three-roomed flat, not too far from the airport.

They managed to save up enough money to furnish it simply and had great fun attending the 'sales'. At one sale, Anna sneezed in the midst of the auctioneer's bargaining; he thought she was nodding her head, and at the end of the morning she found herself in possession of a large, old- fashioned gramophone and a stack of records!

"Oh well, it will liven things up when we have visitors," said Mary. They gave a house-warming party and every one thought it was a great success, but the joy of the occasion was dampened for Anna, when, at the last moment, Tom was called away on duty. But altogether, having a flat was fun, and Anna and Mary felt that they had successfully launched themselves into the adult world.

One day when Anna was on 'stand-by' duty, she was sitting in the cafeteria having a cup of coffee and whiling away the time over a book, when a messenger told her Miss Symonds wanted to see her.

Thinking it must be a call to take over a flight duty, she gladly put away her book and went along to Julia Symonds' office.

"Come in," called out Julia in answer to her knock. "Sit down, I want to have a talk with you."

Anna waited expectantly, half wondering if she had done anything wrong!

"How would you like to fly on 'Comets'?" she asked.

"You mean go overseas?" asked Anna, already bubbling with anticipation.

"Yes," replied Julia. "You, Mary, John and Simeon have done so well that we want to recommend you for promotion. You can attend an 'in- service' course, starting next Monday. It isn't very hard; you have mainly to learn the difference in the layout of the aircraft. Would you like to do that?"

The beaming smile on Anna's face told her all she wanted to know. Anna was thrilled she had been chosen.

So the following week, Anna became a student again; and although she enjoyed the change-over to regular hours, she missed her flying duties and was glad the course was a short one.

On the next Sunday evening, she looked at the notice-board, and to her joy, she found she had been put on the Rome/London flight with Mary, John and Simeon. Tom was also to go along as it was their first trip abroad.

"I must send a cable to my brother," said Mary to Tom, while they were having supper at the airport that evening. "I haven't seen him for years. The last time he had leave, he went to France. I'd like you to meet him," she added.

The Comet was due to take off at twelve o'clock. The transport called for Anna and Mary at quarter to ten and just before eleven o'clock, they reported to the duty-room. There was certainly much more to do than when they were on an 'internal flight'. The list of passengers had to be checked to see if there were any special diets to prepare; or to find out if any invalids or unaccompanied children were coming aboard, who would need special care. There were the usual drink lists and menus, and also lists with details of currency exchanges for the different countries they would pass through; and there were boxes of 'duty-free' cigarettes and drinks that passengers were allowed to buy and take through the customs without paying duty. All was in order and there were no V.I.P.s, invalids or unaccompanied children on the passenger list.

On the plane, they stowed away their personal baggage, checked the amount of food, drinks, cutlery, trays, plates and glasses. Lastly, they walked the length of the aircraft, seeing that everything was spotlessly clean and tidy.

Then the passengers came on board, each one with a numbered boarding-pass. Tom stood just inside the doorway and greeted everybody in the central cabin, and Anna welcomed the First Class passengers entering at the front of the aircraft and showed them to their seats. John, Simeon and Mary stood at intervals along the gangway of the central cabin, making sure that the passengers found their seat numbers and helped them to stow away their coats and hand-baggage. When they were all settled with their seat belts fastened, Mary, Anna and John, standing in different parts of the plane, demonstrated the use of the oxygen masks and life-jackets, while Simeon gave the commentary on how they should be used.

At last all was ready, the doors were closed and bolted, and Tom told the pilot they were prepared for take-off.

However many flights Anna went on, she always felt a thrill the moment they left the ground. Now, as the huge machine hurtled down the runway, she held her breath and waited for the barely perceptible change in noise and the strange feeling of lightness, that told her the pull of gravity had once more been defeated and over a hundred tons of metal had been lifted effortlessly into the sky.

They climbed swiftly and levelled out at about thirty thousand feet; passengers unfastened their seat belts, relaxed and smoked. Tom, Simeon and John attended to the request for pre-lunch drinks and Anna and Mary put down the tables and started to hand round the lunch-trays.

"You know," said a well-seasoned, competent-looking passenger, sitting near the window. "I really think this is the most wonderful way of travelling. I've written a letter and my writing is as smooth as if I were sitting at home at my desk. And now, look at you walking along with all those trays, serving us as if we were in a restaurant on the ground."

Just then, the plane hit an air pocket and gave a great bump. Anna felt the floor drop away from under her and hung desperately on to her tray. But as her feet became firmly fixed on the floor again, for a fraction of a second, the tray remained suspended in mid-air. She did not really let go, but her hands came down with a jerk and the tray crashed on to the empty seat beside the passenger.

"A bit of luck no one was sitting there," said Anna, with a shaky laugh.

Everything had miraculously remained intact, held in the grooves of the cleverly partitioned tray.

"Fasten your seat belts," came the voice of the Captain over the loud speaker. At the same time, the 'No Smoking' signs were lit up in the cabins.

"A bit bumpy," said the seasoned traveller. She was clutching her 'airsick' bag and looking most unhappy. "I don't think I want any lunch, thank you," she added in a muffled voice. "I don't know how you girls serve us at all, being bumped up and down like this. I forgot to take my pill — that's why I feel funny."

"Shall I get you one now?" asked Anna.

"No, thanks," replied the passenger. "It's too late now and, anyway, it will be perfectly all right in a moment."

After about five minutes, the aircraft was again as smooth as if it were stationary and the passengers were told they could unfasten their seat belts and smoke.

"I wish we were staying here," Anna said to Tom, when the plane touched down at Rome airport that afternoon. "I've heard so much about the fountains, the statues and the art galleries, let alone the shops here. I'd love to see them all."

"Be patient! You will one day," said Tom. "But I'm afraid air crew know a lot of cities by name only. I can tell you a dozen places where I've landed and never been farther than the airport. You have to accept that as part of the job."

It was bitterly cold when they at last arrived at London

54

Airport. At first, the Captain thought he was not going to make it. Dense fog had been reported and he had been told he might have to divert to Gatwick as an alternative. But, at the last moment, the fog had turned into a heavy drizzle and it had cleared enough to land.

Anna's thick coat felt like a cotton sheet and the damp bit into her bones as she stood at the top of the steps saying 'good-bye' to the passengers and hoping they had had a pleasant journey.

"Come along," said Tom. "Report to customs; wait for our luggage; then to the hotel. Tomorrow you can contact your brother."

Anna half hoped that Jonathan would be there to meet her, but she had not told him the time of the plane's arrival, and there was no familiar face amongst the thousands of strangers that hemmed her in on every side.

They waited for a long time for the luggage to be brought and then they were given a hair-raising search by the Customs' Officer, who seemed to think that anyone from Africa must be loaded with skins, guns or strange fruit and plants! It was nearly midnight before they reached their hotel and by then Anna felt tired and depressed and utterly miserable with cold.

The next morning she 'phoned her brother. He did not seem so excited to hear her as she had expected.

"How long are you staying here?" he asked.

"Two whole days," said Anna. "When can I see you?"

"I'm afraid not till this evening," said Jonathan, his voice sounding unreal and mechanical over the 'phone. "Tell me where you're staying and I'll call round for you at about seven o'clock."

As she was going away from the telephone booth, the hotel porter called her. "A message for you, Miss," he said. "A Mr. Clinton rang — said he had to go off on family business but would call here at seven-thirty tomorrow evening."

Anna went back to the room she shared with Mary. She opened a window on to the grey streets and the grey sky and shivered as a grey-white snowflake blew in and settled on her. She closed the window tightly and went over to sit on the radiator.

"Thank goodness for this," she said. "I didn't realize it could be SO cold. And no sun — it's difficult to imagine this sort of weather for months on end."

"Let's explore the shops and the Underground," said Mary.

The cold did not seem to bother her. She could hardly believe she was in London, with all the shops, concerts, theatres she had heard so much about. She did not know where to begin. Anna wished they knew someone who could take them around; Simeon and John wanted to go off on their own and the crew had relations or friends to see. But Mary did not care — the world was at her feet!

"Come ON," she said to Anna. "What's the matter with you?"

"Nothing's the matter," said Anna, putting on her coat and gloves. They picked up their handbags and took the lift downstairs.

"Where do you want to go?" asked the friendly porter. "Do

you want a taxi?"

"We want to go on the Underground," said Mary firmly. "To Oxford Street, to see the shops," she added. It was the only street she could remember, having read the name somewhere in an advertisement in a newspaper.

The porter gave them a little map and told them which direction to take.

"Get off at Marble Arch Station," he said. "That's the beginning of Oxford Street and you can walk from there."

They thanked him and pushed open the swing doors. The raw, damp, clammy atmosphere enveloped them as they pulled their coats round tightly and walked quickly in the direction the porter had shown them. They looked up at the Underground sign and walked down some steps and along a passage to the top of a moving staircase.

"Come on," said Mary and gave a little jump on to the top step.

Anna did the same and held tightly to the hand-rail until she found it was moving faster than the stairs! She let go with a jerk and quickly clutched the part beside her, wondering why the railing and staircase could not be co-ordinated! She watched Mary jump off the bottom step and stood petrified as the ground came up to meet her, and then almost fell on her nose when the last stair flattened out and disappeared beneath her!

They both giggled, thinking they had made fools of themselves and that everyone must be staring at them. But no one was looking; no one even noticed a couple of strangers trying to find their way about the big city.

A blast of hot air flattened their clothes against them as they waited for the train to appear through the dark tunnel. The doors opened with a hissing sound and Mary and Anna were pushed back, then swept inside with the surging crowd and sat, bumping and swaying in the stuffy compartment.

They counted four stations, then pushed their way out. Going up the moving stairway did not seem so bad as coming down, but they were thankful to feel the fresh, cold air on their faces as they handed in their tickets and went out of the exit.

"That was quite an experience," said Mary.

"It certainly was," agreed Anna. "But it made me feel a bit queer — let's go back by bus."

"As long as we can find the right bus", replied Mary, looking at the hazardous traffic, which included dozens of buses with different numbers, apparently all going to different places.

"What a lot of people," exclaimed Anna. "There seems hardly enough space on the pavements to walk along; the people look as numerous as ants in the forest!"

Just opposite was a huge store which seemed to cover the whole length of a street. They wandered along and saw others like it; block after block of enormous buildings, and in between, smaller shops and little restaurants.

"Let's go inside one of the big stores," said Mary, as they walked down the street, gazing at the decorated windows.

They pushed through the nearest door and the hot, stuffy air, mingled with the scent and cosmetics, rose up into their nostrils and made them feel dizzy. Their frozen fingers and toes ached as the warmth slowly thawed them back to life. For a few moments, they stood and gazed dumb-founded at the glittering lights and the gaily-coloured counters. They adjusted themselves to the atmosphere and wandered through the Gift Department, the Jewellery, the Book Store; then upstairs through three floors containing every conceivable article of both men and women's clothing; up again, through 'Toys and Games' and finally to the restaurant where they sank down on a chair and ordered cups of coffee.

They looked out of the window, over the roofs of the buildings to the revolving tower of the new Post Office and to St. Paul's Cathedral, a grey dome in the distance.

"We'll never see everything," said Mary, looking at her watch. "It's twelve o'clock already and we've been nearly three hours in one shop — and there's hundreds of them!"

"We'll have to come again," Anna laughed as she rubbed her tired feet together under the table.

They decided to have lunch before they continued their exploration of the London streets. It was a long time before they were served but they were glad of the rest. Afterwards they mingled with the crowd of afternoon shoppers and found themselves pushed and shoved and knocked as they struggled along. They walked in and out of the big stores and wandered round until their eyes were surfeited and they could not take in any more.

All at once, a peculiar light came over the sky and slowly it began to grow dark.

"It's only just after three o'clock," said Anna and she and Mary clutched one another, thinking that the end of the world was at hand.

Suddenly, large white flakes began to drop from the sky

and settle on Anna's coat; she brushed them off and they disappeared into little wet patches. "Snow," she cried excitedly. "Real snow!"

A flurry of white rained down from the sky and Mary tried to catch the flakes in her hand and look at the intricate patterns involved in their make-up, but they melted at the warmth of her touch.

The snow stopped as abruptly as it had begun but the sky became blacker. Suddenly, a wonderland of light lit up the dismal darkness. Anna and Mary stood and stared, forgetting the cold. As well as the street lights, hundreds of tiny coloured lamps were strung across the road above their heads; patterns of ships, aeroplanes, Christmas trees and animals. As they gasped in wonder, they heard a woman say, "I come every year to see these lights. They're here every Christmas-time — have been for years — they only stopped having them during the war."

A clock struck five.

"We'd better think about getting back," said Anna. "Or we won't be ready when Jonathan calls."

"We haven't even bought anything," said Mary. "And now the shops are closing."

"There's always tomorrow, or next time we come," said Anna.

A taxi came by and they decided to take it. This was rather extravagant but they were both shivering with cold and their aching feet would carry them no further!

Jonathan called at the hotel at seven o'clock, bringing a friend for Mary. The joyous re-union Anna had imagined for so long was a disappointment; Jonathan appeared rather cold and distant, and Anna realized they had grown apart.

"So you're an Air Hostess?" he said, when introductions had been made all round. "I thought you'd go on to University and teach or something."

"Oh," she replied. "But you always said travelling was so interesting. I thought you'd be pleased."

"Well, as long as you can look after yourself," he said with a meaningful look. "We've got tickets for the theatre," he went on, changing the subject. "I thought you two girls would like that. There's just time for a meal first; so let's go."

They had an enjoyable evening, but all the time Anna sensed that Jonathan did not seem too pleased to see her. However, when they said good-night, he invited her and Mary round the following evening to his flat.

Anna asked if she could bring Tom. He hesitated a moment.

"I suppose so," he said. "It's a party; one more or less won't make much difference!"

The next day, Anna and Mary visited the Tower of London, St. Paul's Cathedral, and lastly Westminster Abbey, where they saw, hewn on the grave-stones, the names of famous people they had learnt about in their history lessons. They crossed Waterloo Bridge and walked along the Embankment, but decided against taking a boat down the river.

"We'll come back and do that in the warm season," said Anna.

"If there ever is one!" answered Mary through chattering teeth.

They found their way back to the hotel on the Underground and this time it did not feel so strange.

They bathed and changed and waited for Tom. Anna thought he would never come, but he arrived after seven-thirty and they took a taxi to Jonathan's flat.

The room was already crowded when they arrived; serious young men and women were discussing politics and other intellectual topics. The drinks flowed freely; then someone switched on a record-player. This made Anna nostalgic for the battered old gramophone in her flat, so many thousands of miles away.

The talk took on a lighter vein and couples took turns to dance on the fifty-cent space they had managed to clear in the centre of the room. But, for Anna, the evening was not a success. Every time Tom spoke to Jonathan, she could feel her brother's bristling hostility and could sense a barrier building up between them. When it was time to leave, there was a distinct coldness in their goodbyes.

"It's no good, Anna," said Jonathan. "It won't work out. I know!" Those were his parting words, and Anna was relieved to be flying back to Nairobi the next day.

When she reported for duty on her return, Julia Symonds called her into her office. "And how did you enjoy your trip?" she asked.

"It was wonderful," replied Anna. "But it's good to be back."

"I know exactly what you mean," said Julia, smiling.

Chapter 7

NIGHT FLIGHT

The plane took off at eight o'clock in the evening with Anna, Mary, Asha and John as cabin staff. As soon as they were airborne, they started preparing the dinner trays and giving them round to the passengers. The food had been cooked at the airport and was still hot in the containers. While they were trying to make everything look as attractive as possible, passengers kept ringing their bells and asking for pre-dinner drinks and cigarettes. Anna and Mary rushed backwards and forwards as the passengers tendered notes in different currencies and clamoured for change.

"Curried vegetables for the vegetarians," said John, who was in charge of the cabin on this flight "Curried chicken for the others; roast chicken for those who don't like curry."

Anna consulted the list on which were written the passengers' special dietary requests; then she passed round the trays to those in the main cabin. There were many business-men; some taking their wives back to India on holiday; some, obvious tourists, clutching cameras and brochures and binoculars; a few were young students, looking rather baffled with the procedure of fastening and unfastening safety belts, the enclosed space and the number of people on board.

The plane was full and Anna and the others took quite a time to hand round all the dinner trays. Then she took a cup of coffee to the pilot.

"Is this all I'm going to get?" he asked.

"No," quipped Anna. "That's just to keep you awake for dinner!"

"Don't starve me," said the pilot. "We've a long way to go."

"We've got two days off in India," said Anna. "Do you know it well? Were you born there?"

"No, I was born in Kenya," answered the pilot. "But I've still many relatives there. Do you know Bombay?"

"No, I've never been there before," said Anna. "I'm looking forward to seeing it."

The plane touched down at Aden to refuel; it was quite dark and Anna could see the different coloured lights that marked out the runways, taxiing lanes and parking bays. The plane dipped towards the centre of a series of yellow lights and Anna felt the slight impact as the tough tyres touched the ground. The backward thrust of the engines made a tremendous noise as the pilot opened up the flaps and slowed the plane to a walking pace. She watched the marshaller guide the pilot to the parking area, the ends of his batons lit up like two orange flames.

Anna was surprised that the airport lounge was so small; the atmosphere was stifling — there was no air-conditioning; the few slow-moving fans merely stirred the hot, humid air round and round and Anna felt she was sitting in a steam-bath.

Most of the passengers crowded round the tiny 'duty-free' stall which served as a shop, buying transistors, films, cameras and bottles of gin, whisky and brandy. Then, exhausted by the unaccustomed heat, one by one they sank gratefully into the faded, plush arm-chairs. White-liveried Arab waiters collected their complimentary refreshment chits and served them with cold drinks and biscuits.

Anna sipped an orange squash and examined the clocks on the wall, which showed the time in different parts of the world. Here, in Aden, it was eleven o'clock in the evening, the same as in Nairobi; in Bombay, it was two-thirty in the morning; in London, it was eight o'clock in the evening; in Sydney, it was six-thirty in the morning.

"How muddling," thought Anna. "I'll lose some sleep on this trip, but I suppose I'll make it up on the way back. Now, if you travel on round the world, you lose a whole day." She sat back and thought about this. "Fancy losing a whole day of your life," she said aloud.

"What on earth are you talking about?" asked John.

"Well, if you keep travelling the same way round the world, you'll never catch up," said Anna, not making herself very clear.

"No, it's very strange," replied John. "I can never get used to this change of time, and I find it an awful job to work it out sometimes."

"Flight 218 for Bombay is now ready to leave. Will passengers go through Exit B. The transport is waiting to take you to the plane."

Anna picked up a large bag belonging to an old lady.

"Thank you," she said. "It's very kind of you to help an old woman."

"Are you going to India on holiday?" asked Anna, conversationally.

"No, dear, I'm going for good. I'm old now and I've had a good life, but I want to die in my own land, near the place where I was born."

"You're not going to die yet," said Anna, cheerfully, as she helped the old lady up the steps and made sure she was comfortably seated before she left her. She put the bag down on the floor and tried to tuck it under the seat.

"Can't this go on the luggage rack?" asked the the old lady.

"I'm sorry," said Anna. "But it's rather heavy, and if by any chance the plane goes through a bumpy patch, it might fall on someone's head!"

All the passengers were on board and Anna, Mary and Asha walked quickly down the gangway to make sure that every one had their safety belts fastened and that no one was smoking. Then they went to report to John.

John picked up the receiver of the 'intercom' and told the pilot they were ready for take-off.

The Captain started up the engines and taxied slowly down the runway in between the coloured lights. Given the 'all-clear' from the Central Tower, he revved up and the plane sped faster and faster down the runway, stopped, turned, and with a great roar, sped along again at terrific speed until it took off into the blackness and the twinkling lights of the airport were soon far below. Anna could see the ships in the harbour outlined with their lights against the sky, and farther back, the mass of colours which etched out the buildings of the town. Then there was nothing but blackness and the flames of the powerful jets darting out behind.

"What a magnificent feeling," thought Anna. "Here we are up above the world; a hundred and seventy people, flying through the universe, not belonging to time or space."

She pulled aside one of the little curtains and gazed out at the stars; and the milky way looked like a great cloud lying across the heavens.

The ring of a bell called her back, if not to earth, to the inside of the plane! She walked along until she saw a bell lit up above one of the seats. It was seat number 3A, near the front by the window.

"Yes, Sir," said Anna. "Is there something I can get for you?"

"A scotch on the rocks, please, Miss," said a middle-aged business-man.

Anna went to the bar and carefully measured out a double tot, put a few lumps of ice in the glass and carried it on a tray to the passenger. Meanwhile, Mary and Asha walked slowly down the gangway, asking each person if he wanted a 'night-cap'. John went through the folding-door to look after the First Class passengers. A few had whisky or brandy, most asked for Ovaltine, hot chocolate or milk.

About half an hour later, Anna picked up the receiver of the Public Address System and told the passengers she was going to dim the lights.

"There's an individual light just above your heads if anyone wants to read," she said. "But I expect most of you will have a sleep."

She then turned off the main lights and walked quietly down the gangway once more, handing out pillows and blankets, and helping some of the passengers adjust their seats to the 'reclining' position.

Soon all was quiet except for a few desultory murmurs. One or two passengers switched on their reading lights but most of them leant back against their pillows and closed their eyes.

Anna and Mary went to their little galley at the tail-end of the plane and started to sort out the towels, soap and other toilet articles, replacing those that had been used up, replenishing the supply of tissues, hand cream, shaving lotion etc.

All was quiet except for a sigh here and there and a few snores that could be heard above the steady hum of the engines. They could hardly feel any movement and Anna found it difficult to realize they were hurtling through the skies at six hundred miles an hour, thirty thousand feet above the earth.

"How weird it feels," she thought for the hundredth time. "How do you feel, Mary?" she asked in a whisper.

"I feel very strange," Mary whispered back. "Here we are, a hundred and seventy people, mostly all complete strangers, cooped up in a tiny box, speeding together through the universe; so intimate and yet most of the passengers will never see each other, or us, again."

"It makes me wonder about them all," said Anna. "Who are they? Why are they travelling?"

"It feels eery," said Asha, who came along to join them. She shuddered.

"I feel I don't belong anywhere except to this moment. It's as if we were going on for ever. You could never explain the feeling to any one who hadn't been in an aeroplane at night, let alone any one who hadn't been up at all."

68

Just then, the pilot put his head round the door of the crew's cabin.

"Any chance of some more coffee?" he said. "We've got to keep awake you know. It's all right for you girls."

Anna smiled and the cabin door clicked too.

"Come on," said Asha. "Let's make them some coffee. I don't feel very sleepy, do you?"

"No, surprisingly not," replied Anna. "I only hope I don't collapse with tiredness in Bombay. I don't want to sleep all the time and go back without seeing anything of India!"

"India sounds so exciting," said Mary. "Asha, were you bom there?"

"Yes, actually I was, but my family came to East Africa when I was very young and I didn't remember it at all when I came back on my first trip."

They made enough coffee and sandwiches for themselves and the crew. Anna took the tray through to the flight deck.

"Thanks a lot," said the pilot, taking one of the mugs and some sandwiches. "Maybe I'll take you out some time for this!"

Anna stepped softly down the middle of the gangway, trying not to wake any of the passengers, when she heard a sigh coming from one of the seats on her right. She saw a woman reach up and switch on her reading-light. The passenger noticed Anna and smiled.

"Can I fetch you a drink?" Anna whispered, bending slightly towards her, trying not to disturb the two men who were sleeping soundly beside her.

"That would be wonderful," said the woman, gratefully. "I'd love a cup of coffee. I can never sleep on an aeroplane, but I don't really mind much; it's such a wonderful feeling, as if time stood still. Do you ever feel like that? Or are you too busy to think about that sort of thing?" she asked.

"I know exactly what you mean," replied Anna, her young face full of hidden depths.

The passenger nearest the gangway stirred and half turned in his seat. Anna put her hand to her lips and silently went off to the galley to prepare some more coffee. The woman by the window pulled aside the curtain that covered the glass and gazed out into the blackness at the red fire shooting out from the four powerful jets. She was still in the same position when Anna returned with the coffee, piping hot, in a pale blue plastic cup on a matching tray.

"Thank you very much," said the woman, and drew the curtain back again, shutting out the night. She gave Anna a fleeting smile containing a tinge of envy. At her job? At her youth? Anna was not sure.

"Shall I bring you some magazines?" asked Anna, as she turned to go.

"No, thank you," said the woman. "I'll just read my book — or think!"

Anna walked once more to the front ot the plane and back. A man beckoned to her.

"What time do we get in to Bombay?" he asked.

"We land at five o'clock," replied Anna.

"How much sleep do we lose then?" he asked.

"Bombay time is just two and a half hours ahead of ours," said Anna, "So we lose that much, I suppose."

"Ah well," said the man, stretching. "I suppose I'll make it up when I return next week!"

"You have a rest," said Mary when Anna returned to the galley. "I'll take over for a while."

Anna sat down on one of the seats provided for the cabin crew, laid her head back against the foam-filled cushion and closed her eyes. She must have dozed off listening to the steady, monotonous hum of the engines, because the next thing she knew was Asha's hand on her shoulder and a voice telling her it was time to prepare the breakfast trays.

Anna rubbed her eyes and went sleepily into the toilet. She tore open a small packet containing a damp, scented towel and wiped it over her face. Hastily, she patted her hair into place and powdered her face. Now she felt refreshed and wide awake as she heard the sounds of the stirring passengers.

John had already made the tea and coffee and Asha was laying up the trays. They darted down the gangway, saying 'good-morning' and giving the trays to those passengers who were awake, leaving the sleeping ones until the last possible moment. John went into the First Class compartment and returned with a grin.

"Four fried; two scrambled; four omelettes," he said. "It's lucky all the other passengers like boiled!" he added. "Come on girls! Mary and Anna, you do the scrambled eggs; Asha and I will do the omelettes."

First, Anna and Mary put two dozen eggs in the boiling water and set the egg-timer to four minutes; then they started beating up the eggs in readiness to scramble them. Three bells rang all at once. Asha dashed down the gangway. "Three passengers want only coffee — nothing to eat," she said, and made a note of their seat numbers.

For the next half hour the galley and gangway buzzed with activity. Then John was walking along offering second cups of coffee and tea. The passengers were all wide awake now and looking surprisingly tidy after a night lolling back in a seat, fully clothed.

John collected the trays from the forward cabin and Mary and Asha fetched those from the central cabin; Anna carried steaming hot coffee and rolls, eggs and bacon to the crew.

"Last again, as usual," said the pilot. "The least important people, we are!" he pretended to grumble.

Anna smiled. "Well, you've been eating and drinking all night," she said.

"You make me feel I've been to a party," replied the pilot. "Two days off when we get to Bombay — I can't wait!"

An orange dawn was breaking in a cloudless sky, as half an hour later they dropped down effortlessly between the twinkling lights of the runway.

"We are now landing at Bombay airport," came John's voice over the loud speaker. "We hope you have had a pleasant flight. The local time is 5.30 a.m. The ground temperature is 85 degrees Farenheit."

The plane was brought to a halt. Mary, Asha and Anna helped the passengers to gather up their belongings and then stood with John at the top of the steps bidding them 'goodbye'.

It took another half an hour to pass through the Customs and check their luggage before Anna climbed wearily into the aircrew's bus taking them to the hotel.

"We stay at a marvellous place," said the pilot. "Just outside the city, near the sea."

No one spoke as the bus swerved over a bridge and the stench of the river rose in their nostrils. The headlights caught the silhouettes of people lying asleep on the side of the road. The bright lights of the town dimmed and one by one the stars faded, as the sun became brighter in the pale, blue sky and the promise of a fine, hot day was fulfilled.

The transport drew up at a large, modern hotel, set tastefully amidst palm trees, within sight and sound of the sea. As Anna got down, she could hear the waves lapping on the shore. She went to the reception desk and a sleepy porter picked up her luggage and ushered her along to her room, saying she could sign in later in the morning.

Wearily, she undressed and washed, and as the final cloud of night disappeared from the sky, and the sun shone down brilliantly over the Arabian sea, Anna climbed into the comfortable bed and fell into a deep sleep.

Chapter 8

RESCUED IN THE NICK OF TIME

"Change money, money change! Change money, money change!" These words chased Anna like a chain of voices, sing-song; the sounds passing from one person to another, accompanying her as she walked along.

"Dollars — sterling — you follow me! I give you good price! Excuse please — follow me!"

Anna had woken late after the night trip to find that John had gone off with the crew and Mary and Asha wanted to sleep on. So she had decided to explore the city alone. Now she wished she had stayed in the hotel. Beggars thrust their filthy hands under her nose or pushed naked, skinny children towards her, showing running sores on their arms; flies covering their half-blinded eyes; maimed limbs twisted under them. Old people lay on mats in the blazing sun; broken, tatty lean-to shelters of coconut matting covered the roadsides; unkempt women stirred a pathetically small pot of curried vegetables, or rolled out the flat chapatties over a smouldering, smoky fire.

The stench from the open drains filled Anna's nostrils and a sickening nausea overcame her as waves of damp heat rose off the pavement and enveloped her whole body. She walked on blindly with ever-quickening steps, trying to get away from the out-stretched hands, the dirt, the smells, the clamour of voices. She came to an intersection in the heart of the city, where five roads led off in various directions. Taking her life in her hands, she dodged in between cars, taxis, double-decker buses, rickshaws and bullock-carts and found herself on a traffic island, where she stood, hypnotized as the mass of vehicles shot by. Drivers hooted, shouted, cursed and swore; people milled this way, that way; ragged dhotis, silken saris, spotless, white shirts, filthy coloured cottons; all mingled together in one vast microcosm of the city streets.

"Missy, see city — I show you — very cheap — you come!" A horse-drawn tonga drew up beside Anna and the driver beseeched her to step inside. Anna looked at the tom leather seat, the black, bent hood; the driver's gaunt, earnest face, the long-handled whip and the dull-coated bag-of-bones which looked more like a cloth-covered skeleton than a horse.

"Anything to get out of this glaring sun and to rest these aching, swollen feet," she thought, and heaved herself up behind the driver.

"Yes, show me the city," she said.

At the crack of the whip, the weary horse sprang forward at a lolloping trot, only to be pulled up sharply by the driver as a taxi screeched in front of its nose. Anna closed her eyes, thinking her last moment had come, but the tonga lurched forward again and round a corner; another crack of the whip and the horse came to life and clip-clopped along the widening road. Anna clutched her stomach and her insides shook as the springless carriage hurtled along and the wooden wheels threw up the unevenness of the cobbled road.

"You got 'Eengleesh' money? American dollar? Money change? I take you. Very good price!" The driver turned to Anna with a crafty smile. "Special for you, Missy!"

"No!" said Anna firmly. "Show me the city."

"All right! All right!" said the driver. "I show you."

The road was smoother and the horse attained a rhythmic trot. Anna began to enjoy the ride as they came to a wide promenade with the shimmering sea on one side and tall, clean, white buildings on the other. They clattered along until the road left the sea and rose steeply upwards for about a mile towards a small dusty park on the flat ground at the top.

"Look," said the driver, proudly. "The most beautiful city in the world!"

And as Anna looked down, the view made her forget the sights and smells and sounds that had been so vivid such a short time before. She gasped at the beauty of the sweeping curve of the bay; the sparkling sea; the golden sands; a huge ocean liner crossing the horizon and nearer the shore, half a dozen elegant fishing dhows, their sails just filled with the gentle breeze. The brightest-coloured birds she had ever seen flitted amongst the dried-up branches of the nearby trees and the brilliant red of the cotton silk flower shone with a fluorescent light in the dazzling sun.

At the driver's suggestion, Anna got down and ordered a drink at the little stall.

"No fruit," said the driver, as Anna pointed to a delicious-looking piece of water melon. "That make Missy bad inside — run plenty — drink in bottle O.K. No glass. No water to wash glass here. Plenty dysentery."

Anna gratefully gulped down the fizzy orange, drinking directly from the bottle.

"Ice-cream, very good," said the stall-keeper.

"No ice-cream," said the driver.

Anna obeyed with a sigh and climbed into the tonga once more and they jogged slowly down the hill.

"You want to buy? Metal work? Ivory? Silk? Saris? Sandals? I take you — very good price. Shopkeeper my friend."

Before Anna could answer, the driver jerked roughly on the reigns; the horse stopped momentarily and then swerved round a corner and down a side street which led into an alley. It was so narrow that people had to crouch in doorways to save themselves from being crushed against the walls of the tumble-down buildings. The now familiar smell of garbage rose up from the drains and naked children played in the filth of the gutter. The driver stopped outside an open doorway and Anna saw two men squatting on their haunches, an intent look on their faces. Each was chiselling carefully at a small hunk of ivory. The younger man had a shock of long, straight, black hair, which fell over his face, making him shake back his head in a continual rhythmic gesture. The older man had wisps of grey hair of different lengths, which appeared to grow in patches on one side of his head. His grizzled beard curved down his chest and he rested the piece of ivory on its soft bed as he worked. Anna watched, enthralled, as the pieces took shape under the craftsmen's hands.

"Son, father, grand-father, great-grand-father — all in business. Far back — no one remember how far — this man's family always work with ivory."

It must have been half an hour that Anna stood there, forgetful of the filthy surroundings, the desperate poverty of the people, the seething mass of children that now crowded round her, rubbing her skin and touching her hands, her arms, her legs, her clothing. She watched the delicate movements of the craftsmen's hands as they cut and probed and scraped with loving care at the living material before them.

"You like, yes?" said the younger man, at last.

He handed Anna an exquisite carving. It was shaped in the form of a mango fruit, cut in half, but still joined at the back: inside was a model of two bullocks drawing a cart, their driver sitting up in front, flourishing a whip. Every detail was perfect and it had been chiselled from one piece of ivory in front of Anna's eyes; nothing had to be fixed back inside and nothing unnecessary had been taken away. The older man looked up at the beautiful creation in Anna's hands. A faint smile of approval passed over his tired, shrivelled-up dusky skin. He lay down his tools, as, with a final flick, he finished his own master-piece and held it up for Anna to see. She could hardly believe her eyes when she beheld five intricately-carved ivory balls, each one moving freely inside the other.

"The master-craftsman," said the driver. "Son learn many years before he can do such things."

Anna stared in wonder from father to son and saw a look of reverence on their faces as they gazed at their creations.

"Missy want? You got 'Eengleesh' money? American money — I give good price!"

Anna desperately wanted these beautiful things.

"Five pound his — ten pound mine," said the old man, looking up with a cunning smile, his face completely changed.

Not only did Anna not have the money, but she knew she could never afford to pay so much for an ornament, however beautiful it was or however much she longed to possess it.

"I've hardly any money," said Anna, suddenly realizing how true this statement was and wondering if she had even enough to pay the driver.

It appeared that the same thought now crossed the driver's mind and he spoke rapidly to the men in a language Anna did not understand. She heard something like 'air crew' and 'bargain' and then the younger man disappeared into the black depths of the hollow building.

He soon returned carrying a small package, looking round furtively. The old man got up and roared at the crowd of children who were peering into the doorway; he flayed his arms in such a terrifying fashion that the children fled, screaming, to the other end of the street.

"Where you go next?" asked the younger man. "Nairobi? Rome? London? When you go London? Soon? Next week?"

"Next week, I think," said Anna. "Although of course, we're never sure. The schedules might be changed."

"Next week, week after. Doesn't matter," answered the young man. "When you go, take this parcel. Go to Corner Cafe, Hill Street, Soho. Big man at door. You say, 'Give this to Kaka', and hand over package. That's all. Now you go. Take these, no pay." He wrapped up the coveted carvings and handed them to Anna.

"Back to hotel now, Missy," said the tonga- driver. "If anyone ask what in parcel, you say 'present for friend'."

Confused, Anna once more climbed up on to the tom leather seat.

"Hotel, where?" asked the driver.

Anna told him.

"Missy come long way," he said, and he whipped the drooping horse into action and the tonga rattled and bumped its way along a labyrinth of narrow lanes, through the seething masses of starving humanity, until the road suddenly broadened out and Anna caught a glimpse of princely white buildings in the midst of shady trees and vast, well-kept lawns and tidy flower-beds.

"Rich people's houses," said the driver. "Indian princes, business-men."

Turning round the corner, a sorrowful, grey-white hump-backed cow stood still in the centre of the road, contemplating the curb. The driver yelled but the cow refused to move. He jerked the reins to the left and the tonga half mounted the pavement at a crazy angle and edged carefully round the animal before continuing on its way.

"Cow, sacred animal," explained the driver. "Must not touch."

By now, Anna's thoughts were too jumbled to question anything and she was glad when the boneshaking vehicle stopped in front of the imposing doors of the luxurious hotel where the airways staff were staying. The huge Sikh doorman, dressed in a spotless white suit with a large red turban on his head, looked with disapproval as Anna almost fell to the ground, clutching her handbag and her two parcels.

80

"How much, please?" she asked the driver.

"Forty rupees," replied the driver, with an expressionless face.

"Oh no," gasped Anna and opened her bag. Her passport was there, but her purse was gone — she had nothing but a few loose coins!

She was completely at a loss and while she was wondering what to do, the Airways coach drew up at the door — and out jumped Tom!

"Tom," Anna almost cried with relief. "Tom, how marvellous to see you. Why are you here? Listen, I've no money. Can you help me? I'll explain later," she said all at once, before he could get a word in edgeways!

The strain of the afternoon's experience clearly showed in Anna's worried face and Tom wondered what was the matter.

"I've come out in place of Simeon, who has got a bad cold," said Tom, answering one of her questions, while he thought what to do. "I haven't any Indian money on me as I left in such a hurry. Just a moment and I'll change a traveller's cheque. How much?" he said, turning to the driver.

"Fifteen rupees!" the driver mumbled sullenly.

"That's probably ten too much, you old rascal," said Tom. "All right, wait a moment."

He ushered Anna before him through the swing doors into the hotel.

"Sit down a moment and I'll see to the 'tonga-walla'," he said. "You look exhausted," he added. "By the way, what's in that parcel?" He indicated the one she held on her lap.

"It's-er- it's-well-it's some ivory carvings," said Anna, stumbling over her words.

Tom looked at her critically. "And what's in the other parcel?" he asked quietly as she tried to hide it under her handbag.

"I-I-I don't really know!" said Anna, looking down at her feet.

Tom changed some money and went over to Anna, who was now nearly in tears.

"Tell me how you came by that parcel," he demanded, firmly. "How is it you're carrying a parcel around without knowing what's inside?"

Anna did not reply.

"Quickly, come in here," he said and he led her into a corner of the elegantly-carpeted, cool, air- conditioned lounge. Luckily it was empty.

"Tell me before I pay off that cabby," he demanded.

Sobbing with relief, Anna blurted out the story of her afternoon.

"Give me those parcels," said Tom urgently. He grabbed them from her and rushed out to the waiting tonga.

After a few minutes, Anna heard the measured clip-clop of the horse's hooves fading away in the distance. Tom returned empty-handed. He said nothing but opened his wallet and handed Anna a newspaper clipping.

"DRUG AND DIAMOND SMUGGLING RING EXPOSED," she read in large, black letters. "In the early hours of the morning, police raided a cafe in Soho run by a man who calls himself 'Kaka'. Illegal drugs and thousands of pounds' worth of diamonds were found hidden under floor boards and in concealed cupboards. A list of 'carriers' was found, several aircrew amongst them. Although it is believed that many people were innocently implicated, not knowing what was contained in the small packages they were asked to take 'to friends', anyone involved who is employed by an Airline, will automatically be dismissed. The police think that 'Kaka' is the 'master-mind' behind a large smuggling racket..."

A shudder ran through Anna from head to foot and she felt physically sick as she handed the cutting back to Tom. They looked at each other for a long moment. Neither spoke.

"Go and lie down for an hour or so, then I'll take you to dinner," said Tom, after a while.

"The carvings were so beautiful," said Anna in a tiny voice.

"I'll buy you some just the same and just as beautiful," Tom replied. "We'll go and bargain for them, but this time we'll pay for them," he added.

Anna noticed once again the kindly smile crinkle up the corners of his mouth and the wrinkles round his eyes; she gave a great sigh and the loneliness and sickness left her.

Chapter 9

DITCHING IN THE DESERT

Anna was very excited when she heard she was on the Cairo trip; she was to have a day and a half off there, as another crew was to take that plane on to London, and they would follow in the next. Mary, John and Simeon, were to be on the flight; Simeon was the Chief Steward and Anna the 'second', in charge of the galley. The aircraft was a Comet and there were five in the crew.

"Seven men and two girls; not a bad proportion!" said the pilot, who came in as they were reporting for duty an hour before take-off.

"I've heard so much about the pyramids and the sphinx," said Anna, dreamily, staring into space. "I can't believe I'm actually going to set them."

"Just in time before he crumbles away," said the Captain. "The old sphinx is wearing out with the years."

"And riding on a camel or an Arab horse," continued Anna, taking no notice of the interruption.

"Come on," said Simeon. "Or we won't be ready to start on time and then we won't be seeing the pyramids or the sphinx on this trip."

Little did he know the prophetic truth of his words as he set about his duties and gave the cabin a final inspection.

They just had time to tidy themselves up when the passengers started to come aboard. It was midweek and there were only forty-six passengers, including a baby, on the list, instead of a possible seventy.

"We won't be too rushed on this trip," said John to Mary, as they counted out the dinners, stacked the trays in position and switched on the urns and ovens.

Anna stood at the top of the steps at the front of the aircraft, greeted her passengers and helped them find their seats. She had prepared a place for a carrycot as she had been told that the mother and baby were travelling in the First-Class cabin.

Simeon came through and welcomed the passengers on board; John and Mary walked down the gangway, passing round the sweets and seeing that everyone had their seat belts fastened securely. John counted the number of passengers; there were only forty-four; he checked his list again; there should have been forty-six. He reported this discrepancy to the Captain, who relayed a message back to the departure lounge. Apparently the missing passengers — the mother and baby, had been called six times but had not appeared. The aircraft would have to leave without them.

Simeon reported that all aboard were ready for take-off; the steps were just about to be wheeled away, when a young woman came hurrying across the tarmac, accompanied by an Airlines Officer holding a carry-cot. The woman ran up the steps of the First-Class cabin and the Officer handed the carry-cot to Anna.

"This is my wife," he said, introducing the young woman. "We were due to go on leave, but my deputy is ill and I can't

get away until he comes back. The baby is just four months'
old and my wife wants to show him off to his grandmother;
but she almost refused to go without me. I'm sorry we kept you
waiting."

He kissed his wife goodbye and stroked his baby's soft
cheeks.

"Happy landings!" he called out, as he ran down the steps
and stood waving, as the pilot revved up the powerful engines.

Anna gently placed the carry-cot on the table in front of
the mother, picked up the baby and handed him to her to hold
during take-off.

"I've never flown anywhere before without my husband,"
she said, and a look of fear came into her face.

"We'll look after you," said Anna, and for a moment her
heart stood still as she seemed to read a premonition of danger
in the woman's eyes. For a moment neither spoke.

"Shall I make up a bottle for the baby?" Anna asked, pulling
herself together.

"No, it's all right, thank you," replied the woman. "I'm still
feeding him myself."

"Well, just tell me when you want to feed him," said Anna,
"and I'll fix some curtains round your seat so you'll be quite
private."

The woman thanked her and Anna went to the back of the
plane to take her seat ready for departure. Simeon picked up
the receiver and told the pilot they were ready for take-off; the
engines changed their sound to a higher pitch as the great plane
sped down the runway and rose into the clear, blue sky.

It was nine o'clock in the morning and when the plane
had straightened out at a height of twenty-five thousand feet,
Anna and Mary and the two stewards started to take round the
previously prepared breakfast trays. When the passengers had

finished and Simeon and John had served the last cup of coffee, Mary and Anna collected up the trays and stored them away to be taken off at the next airport. They handed round magazines and saw that the passengers were comfortably settled. It was a five-hour flight; refreshments, lunch and drinks would be served before the end of the journey, but for an hour or so the cabin staff would have little to do. After sorting out the linen and seeing everything was clean and tidy in the galley and toilets, they could have a short rest.

The bell rang and Anna walked along to see what was wanted. It was the woman in the First Class cabin who asked for the curtains to be drawn round so she could feed her baby.

"Perhaps you would just put a little orange and boiled water into his bottle," she asked. "Then if he gets thirsty in between feeds, I needn't bother you when you're busy."

As Anna poured a spoonful of specially prepared, clear, orange juice into the bottle of cooled, boiled water, little did she know that this would eventually help to save the baby's life.

It was about eleven-forty-five and Anna was serving the pre-lunch drinks, when she happened to glance out of the window. For a moment, she was so startled by what she saw that she stood rooted to the spot.

"Are you all right?" asked a kindly voice and Anna turned quickly to see an old gentleman looking at her with some concern.

"Yes, thank you," said Anna. "I just felt funny for a moment. We've had rather a busy time lately."

Trying to remain calm, she walked forward and through the door that led to the crew's cabin.

"Ah, where's our coffee?" asked the pilot, without turning

round.

Anna closed the door.

"Come quickly, someone," she said urgently.

"Whatever's the matter? You look as if you're going to faint," said the First Officer.

"Please come quickly — there's black oil pouring out of one of the engines," she gasped out breathlessly.

The engineer immediately got up and walked through to the end of the plane. Anna followed him, trying not to look serious and feeling her face stiffen in a sickly grin as a few of the passengers glanced up as they passed.

One look out of the window was enough for the engineer! Thick streams of oil were pouring from the engine and disappearing in a vapourized cloud, as the plane, undaunted, continued on its way at a speed of eight miles a minute.

"Send Simeon along to see me," said the engineer to Anna, and walked swiftly back to the flight deck.

Anna stood in the galley and noticed that the Captain had illuminated the 'Fasten your seat belts— No smoking' sign, but the passengers had not noticed and she did not know whether to say anything to them or not. Then Simeon walked past her and in a moment she heard his voice over the loud speaker saying, "There's no cause for alarm, but one of our engines has sprung an oil leak. We may have to make an emergency landing, but try not to worry. We have three perfectly good engines and there is still a chance that we may be able to reach our destination. Meanwhile, please extinguish your cigarettes and fasten safety belts tightly; ladies, take off high-heeled shoes and necklaces; gentlemen, loosen your ties."

Anna went along to the mother; she took the baby out of the carry-cot where he was sleeping peacefully, and handed him to her.

"He'll be safer if you hold him in case we come down quickly," she said.

The mother was now in tears. "I knew something terrible would happen," she sobbed. "I never wanted to come on this plane. That's why I was so late. I pretended I had lost my passport. I was hoping you'd leave without us."

"I'll sit beside you," said Anna, soothingly. "We'll be all right, I'm sure."

Suddenly the aircraft shook and there was a series of small explosions.

"Be ready for an emergency landing," came the Captain's voice over the loud speaker. "Nothing to worry about — we often practise this sort of thing!" he added, in a restrained voice. "Bend over, hold your head in your arms and brace your feet against the seat in front."

The plane lost height so quickly that Anna felt as if they were hurtling uncontrollably through the air. As the blinding desert sand came up to meet them, she thought she saw a shimmering sheet of water. She unfastened her seat belt and lurched into the crew's cabin.

"Do we need life-jackets?" she asked. "We're landing on the water."

"There's no water for another thousand miles except perhaps a tiny oasis in a sea of sand," said the Captain drily. "Go back and fasten yourself in — you're looking at a vast mirage. Be ready for the impact — another five minutes and we'll either be in the midst of the Sahara or in the next world. If no one finds us after a few days in the desert, we'll be in the next world anyway!"

Anna scrambled back to her seat, fastened her seat belt and took the baby from his mother, who was now silently weeping. John came along and took two blankets from the rack above and padded them round the baby. Then he handed a blanket to each passenger and told every one to hold it in front of his head like a cushion.

The aircraft straightened out and seemed once more to come under control, as John and the engineer were removing the emergency exit doors. Immediately, the hot air from the desert rose up and enveloped them; clouds of sand were sucked into the plane and the noise from the three working engines was deafening.

"BE READY — NOW!" shouted the Captain. And with a grinding bump, the aircraft hit the top of a sand dune, bounced several feet into the air and crashed down on its side amidst shrieks and cries from the passengers.

A jet of orange flame shot past the windows from the side sloping nearest the ground. Anna unfastened her seat belt and, with the baby tucked under one arm, she helped the mother to the emergency entrance on the far side of the plane. It was well above the ground and John and Simeon rushed up and fixed the long green canvas chute. There was not a moment to lose. Fortunately, no one had suffered more than a few bruises from the impact and the passengers, probably dazed with shock, were surprisingly orderly as they allowed themselves to be quietly shepherded to the opening. They scrambled into the chute and slid silently to the ground. Anna felt the flames grow hotter as the last passenger climbed into the chute.

"Now, you two girls," said the Captain, quietly.

Anna pushed Mary in front of her and then followed, sliding down on to the sizzling sand.

The passengers stood gazing in horror as the aircraft turned into a blazing inferno. Quickly and efficiently, John, then Simeon, followed by the crew, slid down the chute; last of all came the Captain, his hands and face scorched by a tongue of fire.

"Run as fast as you can," he shouted as he reached the ground.

The passengers were shaken into life. Anna, still carrying the baby, took hold of the mother's arm and ran as fast as she could, away from the blazing plane. They crouched behind a high sand dune as, with a great roar, the twisted shell exploded and pieces of metal were flung in all directions.

After a few moments, all was quiet except for the quiet sobbing and groaning of some of the passengers. Anna could hardly believe that they were all alive and no one was seriously hurt.

Suddenly the baby cried, first softly, then louder and louder. Anna realized how hot the atmosphere was and suggested to the mother that she should feed him.

"I can't," said the mother. "Not now. Not yet. Give him some orange juice. Here's the bottle!"

Miraculously, she had somehow clung on to the bottle all through the landing and running away from the burning aircraft.

Anna gave the baby a few drops of the lukewarm liquid and he stopped crying.

"I'd better keep this in case he needs it later," she said to herself.

Then she began to wonder if they would be rescued and how far they were from any human habitation.

The explosions stopped as the plane burnt itself out and all that was left was a mass of twisted metal. After a while, Anna, Mary, John and Simeon joined the rest of the crew, trying to see if there was anything to be salvaged from the wreck. They found a few tins of food and two cans of water, flung a hundred yards from the plane — that was all!

It was four o'clock in the afternoon; the heat was scorching; the light was blinding; there was no shade. Before the crash, the Radio Officer had managed to contact the station in Cairo and he assured everyone that help would soon be on the way. As he said this, the drone of a plane was heard in the distance. It came nearer, faded, came near again and then faded until nothing more could be heard. With it faded their hopes of rescue, and several people sobbed like children.

"He'll come back," said the Captain. "He's just limiting his area of search."

No one answered.

Suddenly a cloud of dust heralded the arrival of a troop of Arabs in flowing white robes. They galloped up on their camels with a lolloping gait, took one look at the crowd and the twisted core of metal and turned away without a word.

About forty people were galvanized into life and ran after them, shouting. The leader turned round. "Wait," he commanded imperiously. "We'll be back!"

Everyone sank down on to the sand again, exhausted. Simeon whispered something to the Captain, who nodded. Then he passed round one of the cans of water. There was barely enough for everyone to take more than a few sips. Anna gave the baby another drink from his bottle — it was now half empty. Someone saw a few scrubby cactus plants and crawled towards them, trying to break off one of the thick leaves; but the prickles tore his hands and he soon gave up the idea.

The sun beat down mercilessly. They sat waiting, not speaking. A few of the men took off their shirts and rigged up a makeshift shelter for the mother and baby. The baby cried and this time the mother fed him until he fell contentedly asleep in her arms. Anna sat by her side, her mouth and tongue swollen with dryness, murmuring words of encouragement.

As the day dragged on, her thoughts turned to Tom. In her weakness, his face appeared before her blurred and distorted.

"Tom," she called silently, and the image disappeared. "I'll die if I don't see you again. But then I'll only not see you again if I die. Will you mind if I disappear forever?" she rambled on, half delirious.

"What's that?" said the Pilot. "Who's disappearing forever.?"

The sound of his voice brought Anna to her senses.

"What on earth was I saying?" she lisped, unable to contain her swollen tongue within her cracked lips.

"Just rambling," answered the Captain.

The sun began to lose its fierce strength and was slipping

over the horizon when a cloud of dust heralded the noiseless return of the camel caravan. There were about twenty camels and the leader made signs for as many people as possible to mount — the rest would have to start walking and change places with the riders at intervals.

The mother was helped on first, and her baby lifted up to her; then Anna, with Mary holding on behind; then the rest of the women and the elderly. They never knew how far they travelled as they wended their weary way all through the starry night as the welcome cool turned to bitter cold. They rode and trudged like a long line of refugees fleeing from their homeland to happier climes.

In the early hours of the morning, as the Eastern sky turned golden, the wandering caravan arrived at a tiny oasis in the midst of the endless wilderness. The searching plane had seen them and they had been rescued in the only possible way — by camel caravan taking them to the base of a Desert Army Motorized Unit, where twenty vehicles awaited with water and iron rations, to drive them the hundred miles to the nearest airstrip. There, two Dakotas were standing by, ready to take them back to Nairobi.

At the Airport amongst the blur of faces, was Tom! He rushed forward to greet Anna and stroke her matted hair; tears welled up in his eyes as he put his arm round her and escorted her through the crowd of photographers and journalists to the waiting car.

"Anna," he said in a voice charged with emotion. "Anna, you've come back to me!"

A month later, Anna received the following letter; similar citations had been sent to Mary, John and Simeon, and to the members of the Comet crew.

From

The Permanent Secretary,

The Ministry of Civil Aviation.

Dear Miss Lumwaji,

The Minister of Civil Aviation has asked me to express his thanks and admiration for your exemplary conduct when the aircraft in which you were serving as a stewardess crashed in the Sahara Desert.

It is understood that you did everything possible to allay the fears of the passengers, escorting them from the burning aircraft and afterwards doing all you could for their comfort under the most trying conditions.

The Minister appreciates your selfless devotion to duty.

A copy of this letter has been sent to the Manager of your Airline.

It was signed by the Permanent Secretary himself.

Chapter 10

THE LETTER

After her gruelling adventure, Anna was glad to be sent home for a week's leave. She had a happy reunion with her family and did her best to allay their fears for her safety by saying little about her recent experiences and a lot about the interesting places she had seen and the people she had met. Of course they were delighted to hear about her meeting with her brother, Jonathan.

She soon recovered completely from her ordeal in the desert and helped her mother with the household chores and played games with her younger brothers and sisters. She returned, much refreshed, longing to see Tom and tell him about her leave.

She reported at the Airport and saw she was 'on call' for the next twenty-four hours. She decided to go and see if Tom was in his office and let him know she was back. She went upstairs and knocked on the door; a clerk answered and said that ,'Mr. Clinton was not available'. He would give no further information.

Perplexed and anxious, Anna went downstairs again, intending to go to the canteen for a cup of coffee but, as she passed her 'pigeon-hole', she noticed a letter. The post-mark was 'ENGLAND'; the writing, in black ink, was strong and masculine.

Anna knew instinctively it was from Tom, although he had never written to her before. With trembling fingers she tore open the envelope. "Oh dear," she said aloud. "I've spoilt the stamp — it's a new kind too — my brother would have liked it!"

As she read, the skin on her face tightened; a great lump gathered in the pit of her stomach and another rose to her throat; she felt physically sick.

"Anna dear, I cannot see you again," wrote Tom. The writing blurred before her eyes. She blinked and read on. "I was offered a job here as Chief Training Steward. I had to make a decision and I feel sure that, in time, you will agree it was the right one. Please try to understand. Tom."

Her lips twisted in a ring of pain as she re-read the words slowly, letting each syllable sear itself on her brain. She sat perfectly still for a long time. Then she folded the letter carefully and put it in her handbag. She would always keep it. It was the only letter she had ever received from Tom — and there would be no more. Mechanically she picked up her bag and walked out of the building. She saw a bus coming along, travelling in the direction of the city. She stopped it and blindly pulled herself on board.

It was the physical hurt that bewildered her; she could not understand why she felt so bruised, as if some one had hit her all over inside. She wondered why she felt no urge to cry.

"Fares please!" called the conductor.

She handed her money to him without looking. The bus started off.

"You can't go any further, Miss, unless you want to go back where you came from," the bus conductor shouted from the entrance.

Anna had not noticed that the short drive into town was over and the bus was standing in the depot.

She got up and walked to the exit.

"Are you all right?" asked the conductor as she got off.

"Yes, I'm all right," she answered dully.

She walked slowly along the main street, looking in the shop windows but noticing nothing.

"Oh the pain," she kept thinking. "Why does it hurt so?"

Her unhappiness reached a depth she had never known; her shoulders drooped as she walked along — she did not even seem to have the strength to hold herself upright.

She did not know how long she walked that day; she felt a desperate need to be amongst people but she wanted to avoid anyone she knew. All of a sudden, she was utterly exhausted. She called a taxi and gave the driver the address of the flat.

"Is this the place, Miss?" asked the driver.

"Yes, thanks," she said. "How much?"

She got out and handed him a ten shilling note, and walked away without even bothering to wait for the change. She fumbled for her key and let herself in. As she pushed open the door of her bedroom, she noticed a list of 'duties' she kept pinned on the wall. It was out of date, but it reminded her that she was 'on call' and she should not have left the airport, or at least she should have told someone exactly where she could be found at any moment.

Tom's letter had sent everything out of her mind. She hoped she had not been needed. She threw herself down on the bed and looked round the room. Everything seemed dull and colourless. The pretty pink and green curtains and bedspread she had chosen so carefully, the sheepskin rug, the shaded reading-lamp — all seemed like the empty trappings of a stage-set at the end of an unsuccessful play. An agonizing loneliness overcame her and she buried her face in the pillow.

There was a loud knock on the door.

"Come in," she called, lifelessly.

"Anna, Anna, where have you been?" cried Mary. "Asha couldn't go on duty because she had ear-ache and you were supposed to be 'on call'. The transport came here to fetch you, but you weren't in. Why didn't you leave a message where you were going? No one could find you, and in the end Julia had to go herself. It was the 717 Flight to Rome, with a three-day stop-over. You would have enjoyed that."

"I forgot I was 'on call'. I went into town," replied Anna.

"You will be in trouble," said Mary, looking at Anna's dishevelled appearance. "Are you all right?" she asked. "You don't look too well. I'll make some tea and bring it along. Then you'd better go to the Airport and report to Julia's deputy."

Anna drank the tea gratefully. She half wanted to tell Mary about the letter, but she felt she could not talk about it — not just yet anyway.

She got up and looked in the mirror, patted her hair into place and went out. She caught a bus to the airport and went along to the 'Waiting Room' where the stewards and stewardesses who were 'on call', or waiting to report for duty, were sitting around talking. By now they had all heard about Anna's absence.

"You'll be dismissed!"

"You're in for it!"

"You'll have a good telling off and all privileges stopped for a month!"

"Just because you 'ditched in the desert', you can't go a.w.o.l.!"

Anna could not bear the clamour which surrounded her and rushed out of the room.

"Whatever's the matter with her?" said one.

"Lovesick, I expect," answered another. "Leave her alone — she'll get over it, but Julia *will* have something to say when she gets back!"

"If only everyone would leave me alone and let me die!" thought Anna, as she slowly made her way up to Julia's office, not quite knowing whom she would find there.

"I'd better find out what's going to happen. If only Julia herself was here, I could talk to her," she thought. Anna knocked on the door.

"Come in," called Julia.

Puzzled, Anna let out a sigh of relief and opened the door. "I thought..." she began.

"Yes," answered Julia, knowing what was in Anna's mind. "I didn't have to go after all. Hilda was in and said she'd go as she had an extra flight to make up anyway. But what's the matter, Anna? Aren't you well? Why didn't you come and tell me and I could have found someone else to take over your duty?"

"I forgot," said Anna, looking at the floor.

"That's not like you, Anna. I don't understand. You've done so well and after the way you conducted yourself when you had that forced landing I was thinking of putting your name forward for training on the Super VC 10's. You'd better come and sit down and tell me what happened to you."

Anna closed the door and sat down on a chair facing Julia. She did not speak.

"Is something very wrong?" asked Julia, in a gentle voice.

"Yes," answered Anna, flatly.

She took the letter out of her bag and handed it across the desk. Julia took the letter and read the brief contents. She looked up and Anna saw sympathy and understanding in her deep, brown eyes.

"I want to die! I want to die!" cried Anna. "What shall I do?"

"When something like this happens, you do die a little," replied Julia, handing back the letter. "But you'll live again. The pain will lessen and fade, and one day you'll be able to look back with tenderness at the happy times you've had. Then you'll find the ache has almost gone from your heart."

Anna took the letter and held it in her hand; somehow the feel of the thick notepaper gave her a strange sense of comfort.

"But I can't forget him! I'll never forget him! It will never be the same again," said Anna.

"You're right! It will never be the same again," replied Julia. "But you'll have to forget him. It's a one-way journey, child."

"But why did he just write — why didn't he tell me when he last saw me?" said Anna, tightly clutching the crumpled white paper.

"Men don't think the same way as we do. They hate scenes and emotion. For Tom, this was the easiest way."

"But there was so much I wanted to say to him. If I had only known the last time that I wasn't going to see him ever again, at least I could have said some of it."

"At least the last time was happy, wasn't it?" said Julia, trying to find a way of comforting the girl in her distress.

"But, this way — it's like some one dying suddenly. There's so much I wanted to discuss."

"In a relationship like that there always would he. Even if you had had your 'last time', as soon as you had said 'good-bye' you would think of things you had forgotten to say. That's how it should be. If ever there had come a time when you had nothing to say, the friendship would have ended anyway."

"But won't he even miss me? In the letter, he never even said he was sorry. Won't it hurt him at all?"

"That's another difference between men and women; men don't like to express their feelings. Of course it will hurt him, but he'll be able to forget you in his work or when he's doing something that interests him; whereas you will be thinking of him all the time for a while, even when you're seeing a film, reading a book, meeting other people — even when you're supposed to be working," she added with a smile.

"Do these things mean more to us? Do we feel more than men?" Anna asked.

"I don't know if it means more or if we feel more intensely, but I do know that men can put things to the back of their minds and concentrate entirely on what they are doing. Maybe, in that way, they are stronger than us."

Anna buried her face in her hands.

"Oh, help me, help me!" she groaned.

102

After a few minutes, she looked up. "I can't even cry," she said.

"No, your feelings are too deep for tears. They'll come later, and then you'll start to recover. No one can really help you at the moment — you must bear the pain, the agony, by yourself. I can only assure you that the wound *will* heal and that it will have all been worthwhile."

"It seems odd to look in the mirror and see I don't look any different. You'd think it would show in my face," said Anna.

"It shows in your eyes, my dear." There was a pause. "You'd better go now," said Julia. "But you can come back and talk to me any time. Try to keep busy — it helps a little — and don't feel bitter."

Anna gave a sad little smile. Seeing the look of compassion on Julia's face, she wondered if she had gone through the same experience. Then she remembered the incident of the scrambled eggs and the look of shared amusement between Tom and Julia. She remembered the intense moment of jealousy she had felt. She said no more, but got up slowly and went out of the room.

She went down to the cafeteria and ordered a cup of tea and a sandwich. She gulped down the tea, but the sandwich tasted like sawdust; it stuck in her throat and nearly choked her. She wandered on to the tarmac and saw a huge jet come in to land, turn and taxi along the runway. She watched it slowly come to a standstill and saw the steps being wheeled up to the exit. She imagined the passengers unfastening their seat belts and gathering up their belongings. She saw the door open and the Stewardess standing at the top of the steps, saying 'good-bye' to the passengers as they walked stiffly towards the terminal buildings.

Another plane was starting up and the sudden roar of the engines startled Anna. She looked over towards it. Where was it going? Rome, Paris, London?

"Fasten your seat belts and no smoking please," she found herself saying.

All at once, Anna realized that for nearly five minutes, she had not been thinking of Tom. She felt guilty to have forgotten him so soon, even for a moment. Her heart dropped like a lump of lead and the hurt returned and she felt sick and ill again. Her grief was so intense that she did not even notice that the plane had taken off. Now she saw it flying back across the airstrip and rising higher and higher until it was a tiny speck in the distance. A picture flashed across her mind of herself as a small girl watching her brother fly off to a foreign land. Once again her heart rose with the plane as it soared into the air.

"Karachi, Calcutta, Bangkok, Singapore — maybe New York, Moscow, Hong Kong, Tokyo," she thought. There was no doubt her job was exciting — the future was bright — she would travel and meet people and see new places.

"Maybe I'll fall in love again one day," she thought. "But there'll never be anyone like Tom. Perhaps I'll get married and have a family, but before that I want to see the world."

She turned and walked back towards the office buildings. She had decided to ask Julia if she would still consider recommending her for training on the Super VC 10's.

www.ingramcontent.com/pod-product-compliance
Lightning Source LLC
Chambersburg PA
CBHW051433150726
48000CB00005B/2086